To dear Lisa,
This means that I
get a free copy of
yours!
Best wishes
— Tim
May '96.

LETTERS TO FRANCESCA

OCTOBER, 1984–OCTOBER, 1994

Tim Richards

ALLEN & UNWIN

First published in 1996 by
Allen & Unwin Pty Ltd
9 Atchison Street, St Leonards, NSW 2065 Australia

National Library of Australia
Cataloguing-in-Publication entry:

Richards, Tim, 1960– .
    Letters to Francesca: October, 1984–October, 1994.

    ISBN 1 86373 993 9.

    I. Title.

A823.3

Set in 10/13pt Caslon by DOCUPRO, Sydney
Printed by Australian Print Group, Maryborough, Victoria

10 9 8 7 6 5 4 3 2 1

Leave everything
Leave Dada
Leave your wife leave your mistress
Leave your hopes and your fears
Sew your children in the corner of a wood
Leave the substance for the shadow . . .
Set out on the road.

André Breton, *The Surrealist Manifesto*

Contents

Days without violence

Because people believe what they read in trashy magazines, they expect me to resent my mother. Nothing could be further from the truth. If there is one thing in my life that I resent, it's the distortive influence of clichés like 'the wisdom of hindsight'.

Where is the wisdom in hindsight? Hindsight is an intrusion. Hindsight is arrogance worn like a miner's lamp, a narrow beam of light directed for a specific purpose. Why should hindsight's view be considered authoritative? If hindsight was so clever, it would set itself the task of providing accurate weather predictions instead of trespassing on the privacy of a lost moment.

When the merchants of hindsight invite me to join the condemnation of my mother, I upset them by refusing to alter the facts to suit their preconceptions. I tell them that their theories don't interest me. I will describe the events of my childhood only as they are impressed upon my memory.

Inevitably, I picture Mother waltzing between the kitchen and her study, swaying and cavorting like someone dribbling an imaginary basketball, baulking phantom opponents, never two steps in a straight line. Her head would be full of inspirations, wild ideas that needed to be danced out. She might dance for hours at a time, unreachable, sweat streaming down her face, her mouth twisting as she spewed out song lyrics, or numbers, or incomprehensible phrases. She could be in tears. All this, she told us, was the hallmark of her genius. She could only create when she was caught up in pure joy, and she tried to organize her world so that nothing would interfere with these moments of joy. She never once doubted that what she was giving us was the secret of exaltation.

Standing in the entrance hall at Netherby was a blackboard that was central to Mother's experiment in behaviour modification. A sign written in sky-blue chalk pronounced **DAYS WITHOUT VIOLENCE**, and the total below was adjusted each day so that it might read '**36 (Previous Record: 82)**'. Mother had based this experiment on the **DAYS WITHOUT INJURY** signs she remembered outside industrial plants, and her sign operated on a roughly similar principle.

If Johnny and I went fifty days without wrestling, kicking or punching each other, we were rewarded with a new book. It was a ploy. Mother didn't really care about the harm that we did to each other. Her sign was only intended to discourage us from *reporting* harmful acts. She didn't want her work to be interrupted with calls to adjudicate.

Hair always had a special importance. Mother had long, raven locks, the most gorgeous hair that I've ever seen. During the day she tied it up in a bun, with just a ringlet or two allowed to dangle enticingly beside her ears. At night, she would let her hair fall. She brushed and she brushed, the most wonderful repetition, and our greatest thrill was to be allowed to brush her hair.

For all her vanity, Mother was brutally unpredictable with our hair. I might wake to find her above my pillow with her scissors, or else I'd peer through the kitchen doorway to see Johnny's wild protests as mother used his sandy locks as a means to explore some radical new geometry. If you had seen her cutting our hair, you might have thought her cruel, and I'll admit to being disconcerted by Mother's ambushes, but her peculiar sense of hair design never bothered us. We had been conditioned to accept untidiness and unpredictability. Certainty or reliability would have terrified us.

Mother told us that she earned money writing articles for mathematical and philosophical journals. Because our father had sabotaged her career, she couldn't get her work published in Australia unless she published under a pseudonym. But mostly she translated the articles into French or Spanish to facilitate their publication in European or Latin American journals. Mother was always writing, elbows tucked in, guardedly looking over her shoulder, frightened that a masked scholar would burst through the door and abduct her theory of existential ahistoricality.

I don't ever remember her telling us that she had inherited money. Only the house. Her father had built Netherby, and she had lived in the house when she was a girl. She told us that the house had been left to her when her parents were killed in a light plane crash in Kenya. Mother hardly ever mentioned money, and we probably assumed that everyone had gardeners and cleaners as a matter of course.

During the morning, mother would instruct us in mathematics, philosophy, and literature. After we had finished our study tasks, we were free to do as we liked: to draw, read, or play in the vast grounds of the property. We would look up to see Mother sitting on the balcony, staring out over the bay, giving shape to some new definition or aphorism. We never thought of ourselves as prisoners or captives. We were only captive to the extent that we were Australian.

Australia is a captive nation, Mother told us, ransomed off from the Brits to the Yanks. After a time, hostages forget that they are hostages, which is precisely the point when they begin to think like hostages. This house is a republic. The slavery of mind stops at the front gate.

I remember wanting to play with other children. Sometimes we heard them call to us from over the fence, and we called back, but to actually play with them was out of the question. We knew that we would be contaminated.

My brother Johnny gave up sleep after a run of bad dreams. He was eleven or twelve, and he decided that sleep was more trouble than it was worth. For several weeks, he suffered from dreadful fatigue, but after that his metabolism seemed to adjust. Johnny used to say that insomnia was like a muscle, the less he slept, the less he needed to sleep. At night he read, gazed up at the stars, or painted. Sometimes I'd wake to hear him discussing things with Mother, talking into the early hours. Johnny would talk with her, and brush her hair—thousands of long, smooth strokes. I think that it was the extra time that he spent with her then, brushing her hair and talking while I slept, that made Johnny Mother's favourite.

Mother detested all institutions and institutionalized practices. She warned us against physicians, hospitals, psychiatrists, banks, insurance companies, churches, and government. More than anything, she loathed schools. She said that schools were established to set limits on possibility, and to restrain sexuality. She said that the primary business of a school is to infect the world of knowledge with the knowledge of mediocrity. The secondary business of a school is to contaminate the outer world with the mediocrity that passes as knowledge. She said that schools were a red carpet rolled out to honour the unexceptional.

Neither Johnny nor I ever thought to question the definition of terms like captivity, deprivation, intellectual freedom, genius, or madness as they related to our predicament. Mother made sure that she had defined them in ways that championed her seismic intelligence. She thrived on paradox. Contradiction only became problematic for her if she needed to explain the necessity or usefulness of contradictory utterances. On the one hand, she wanted to live in relaxed coalition with contradictory assertions. On the other, she needed to obliterate contradiction to support her intellectual denial of mysticism. If we had been older or more independent we might have asked what dance, poetry, and the refutation of time were, if not a form of mystical engagement. But we didn't ask. We were too accustomed to her amazing capacity for reversals and revisions. She was a master of *ad hoc* rationalization.

Everybody asks about the eggs. It never occurred to us that mother only knew how to cook eggs, because she turned her deficiency into a theory that gave eggs pre-eminence in the diet of an intellectual. Poached eggs for analytical thought. Fried eggs for creativity. Hard-boiled eggs for persuasive argument. Scrambled eggs to fashion the cross-fertilization of disciplinary fields. If we ate bread or toast, it was only to diffuse the dangerous potency of the eggs. We ate cereals and fruit to give the eggs something to operate on. Any slowing of our intellectual activity was attributed to an inferior strain of egg.

Not so long ago, a doctor suggested to me that she fed us eggs because she had a paranoid fear that someone would try to poison her. I can't recall Mother being concerned about poisoned food. What really worried her was that someone might try to poison our thoughts and memories.

We were taught to be wary of the gardener, the cleaning woman, the woman who ran errands, the milkman, the baker, the postwoman, the meter reader, Mormon missionaries, scouts, and insurance salesmen. They were agents. They were opportunistic purveyors of mediocrity. Mother told us that she only left our father when he revealed himself to be an agent.

Your father, she told us, was an apologist for institutions. When they made him Professor, he straightaway turned into one of those old Greeks who were terrified by anything that seemed irrational. Some of those Ancient Greek mathematicians were driven to murder and suicide by their inability to rationalize the square root of 2. You can't live with someone who lives in fear of approximates and approximation.

We had no television or telephone. We had no clocks or calendars. Time was an enemy. Of all the agents, time was the most malevolent. We were taught that death and decay weren't the work of time, but the consciousness of time.

Mother's disdain for chronologicality was behind her encouragement of our most sensuous activity, dance. We danced so that we might hover oblivious to a history constructed out of events, presences and crucialities. Mother taught us that dance and sex were the only points where mind and body met in pure exchange, but I don't recall her explaining sex so thoroughly as she explained dance, or the pure poetry signified by the square root of 2.

A new grammar displaced the new geometry which had displaced the most recent algebra. None of Mother's innovations made much sense, but it was the beauty of their senselessness that we clung to. On one day we could be entirely committed to a version of English where nouns were replaced by numbers. This, Mother argued, would enable us to engage the specificity of spatio-temporal relations the way the Aborigines had. Yet, just a few days later we would be taught to be suspicious of numbers, that numbers (which implied that more than one instance could exist of the one thing) were an anathema to nature. Numbers and nouns could only exist where specific details had been overlooked or distorted. Yet numbers were soon restored to favour when Mother adopted the notion that nature, as an intellectual construct, was itself unnatural.

I remember spending the latter portion of my teenage years as a case study, a human inkblot. I was entirely cut off from Mother, and rarely saw Johnny or my father. All the stories and poems that I had written were taken off to be dissected by forensic psychiatrists. If every absence implied an absent father, every downbeat signified the heavy-footed presence of an egg-eating Queen Lear. My childhood was made and unmade in front of me. My memories were corrected like school history assignments.

Several times since, I've tried to read my poems as poems, to ignore their so-called coded intimations of tyranny, yet I am unable to reinstate the innocence that has been stolen from them. The doctors' incessant question, Did you love your mother? runs through my head on a loop. When I replied in a way that didn't suit them, they would answer, sagely, Of course, you didn't know any better.

I remember the warm summer evenings when the windows were thrown wide open, and the breeze would carry the sound of trains or traffic or children splashing aimlessly in their backyard pools. That's when we would play board games where the object of the game was to land on a square which directed you forward to a square which directed you back to the original square, and so on, *ad indefinitum*. *Ad indefinitum* was a favourite phrase of Mother's. When one or the other of us grew tired of shifting our piece backwards and forwards between the two squares, she reminded us that the idea of infinity has its basis in a binary opposition that is essentially mystical. We lived in a world made meaningful by definite action and commitment. Mention of the infinite was to be treated with contempt. When my deprogrammers referred to these games as a Sisyphean cruelty, I tried to convince them that Johnny and I never tired of the games. We would often seek them out for entertainment during Mother's phases.

Mother's worst phase came not long before the final crisis. She became fixated with the idea of a champagne cork halted in flight, and took to whirling around the library in fast, decreasing circles, trying to fuel the formation of a theory. At one point she got so dizzy that she hammered face-on into a wall and knocked out a tooth.

Not long after, I saw her sitting at a table making minute notations on a large sheet of paper. From what I could see, they were more like hieroglyphs than mathematical symbols. She wrote furiously, and when she finished writing she gazed at the page for more than an hour. I left the room. When I came back, Mother was staring out the window, and her sheet of notes was gone. Later, Johnny told me that he'd watched her tear the sheet into long strips. She rolled each strip into a thick scroll. There were ten or eleven of these scrolls. She made a mark on the outside of each and sealed the end down with glue, before arranging them into some kind of order. Then, one after the other, she placed each scroll in her mouth, chewed, and swallowed.

Besides books and intellectual journals, our only knowledge of the world outside Netherby came in the form of letters and postcards sent by my mother's sister Madeleine. My aunt had married an American journalist and settled in Baltimore. Though they had three children, it seemed to us that my aunt and uncle did little but travel. She sent us postcards of ruined Inca cities, gondolas in Venice, paintings by Edvard Munch, and photographs of film stars like Marlon Brando.

Aunt Madeleine wrote of cinema and television, orchestras and jet travel, and Mother loved to read her sister's letters out loud so that she could provide a vehement critique as she went. My aunt would tell us how beautiful her blonde daughter Catherine was now that she was a young woman. Aunt Madeleine and Uncle Scott spent fifteen thousand dollars on orthodontistry so that Catherine would have the most perfect smile in Maryland. Johnny was very taken with the thought of his cousin. He would often interrupt Mother as she was reading Aunt Madeleine's description of a family trip to ask, Does it mention Catherine?

Once, when Johnny mentioned that he would like to travel with his American cousins, Mother got furious and told him that he was a fool, that all these travels were just a figment of her sister's imagination. She told us that Madeleine's marriage had collapsed, and that she lived alone with her children in some godforsaken caravan park on the Gold Coast. Mother said that Aunt Madeleine's real name was Judy. She said that her sister pretended to have all sorts of glamourous adventures, and perfect American children, but really she was just another victim of mediocre thought and ambition.

If I was astonished by this turn around, Johnny was devastated. He told me that Mother was jealous of her sister, and that Aunt Madeleine's letters were too vivid not to be true. Why would Mother have read and discussed the letters with us if she had known that her sister was lying?

Early one morning, while I was asleep, Mother sent Johnny to fetch a favourite brush from her bedside drawer. Misunderstanding her instruction, Johnny opened the wrong drawer. Inside, he discovered a stack of unmarked European postcards, along with airmail envelopes of the type that Aunt Madeleine used for her letters. Johnny would have been nearly seventeen then.

What I remember most vividly from the two or three days that Johnny was missing was Mother's ceaseless, agitated muttering. I remember her grasping my upper arm, Where did he go? Did you see him go? And the only thing that I could think of was that he had been taken by a gardener or a baker, that he'd been claimed by one of Mother's agents, because it was unthinkable that Johnny would have left of his own volition, that he could have run away. Johnny was Mother's favourite. Why would he want to go? I was the one who didn't matter. I was the one who needed sleep.

I remember the doctor telling me to accept things that I couldn't accept. He told me that my father had always loved us. My father had always searched for us.

To have believed what the doctor told me to believe would have been like saying that my mother was bad, or that my mother didn't have our best interests at heart, and I knew that my mother loved us.

I was told that I would be confused by a lot of things because wrong thoughts, and wrong patterns of thought had been placed in my head, and that I would need to be taught to look at the world the way ordinary people looked at the world.

No one tried to understand me when I said that I didn't want to think like an ordinary person. I clearly remember one doctor asking me to repeat something I'd said so that she could make a note. I told her that ordinary people were hostages to the ordinary. Ordinary people are like the worst kind of Americans; the wannabe Americans, the pseudo-Americans.

For a long time I refused to speak to my father because he said that he was American.

Because I refused to speak to him, my father sent me a list of 'facts'. He said that he had never done anything to harm my mother's career. He had never been an academic. He had never been employed by an Australian university. He was a journalist who lived in Baltimore. He had married my mother in Australia and taken her back to the United States. I had been born in the United States. He told me that my mother had never lived at Netherby when she was a child. She hadn't even lived in Melbourne. He said that when he met her she was living in a suburb of Brisbane. He said that she'd taken Johnny and me when she received her inheritance. He said that she'd suffered a breakdown when her parents died. He said that I had an older sister named Catherine.

I sent my father back a letter saying that he was acting just like an agent would. I returned the American birth certificate ripped into fifty pieces. I accused my father of pretending to have an American family in order to further his career as a university professor.

Not many people my age can remember the first time that they watched television, but I can. I was thirteen years old, and my mother was being interviewed. I remember that she tried to convince the interviewer that there was a second spectrum of light, a set of colours imperceptible to ordinary vision. Past and future events were encoded within this spectrum. Access to the second spectrum would enable you to travel through time. My mother offered to supply the television station with her knowledge of the second spectrum if they would reunite her with Johnny.

I don't actually remember her brushing her hair, but that's what everyone else remembers. They will tell you how shocked they were to see a woman casually brush her hair while being interviewed about the abduction of her children. People focussed on her hairbrushing because they were envious of her beautiful hair, and had to rationalize their mean, mediocre thinking.

No one paid any attention to anything my mother said. She told the judge that he wasn't entitled to judge her because he was a tool of the social apparatus that she had rejected, but he judged her anyway. The prosecutor asked her what she hoped to achieve by holding her boys captive, and she said that she had achieved everything that she had set out to achieve. Her boys understood the awful power signified by the square root of 2.

I wasn't permitted to see my mother until I turned eighteen, by which stage I was more confused than I had been as a child juggling contradictions at Netherby. She had stopped dancing, but she still made discoveries, and tried to convey the importance of those discoveries to the nurses. She called me Johnny, and after a time I stopped trying to correct her. She loved to reminisce about the nights when I would brush her hair till dawn. Her hair was still beautiful, and I could see that the nurses loved to brush her hair for her just as we used to. She would badger me to recall her aphorisms.

But you've forgotten the one about creativity, she'd say.

Only creativity releases us from agency, I told her.

Three years ago, the French Government bestowed the Legion of Honour on a 'remarkable Australian philosopher and mathematician' named Christine Marker. We discovered that Christine Marker was one of many pseudonyms my mother had used when she contributed papers to academic journals in the early 1970s. After the award, the same universities that Mother had always distrusted and despised offered her professorships and honorary doctorates. It was a real pity that she was so far beyond telling them what she thought of institutions and institutionalized thought.

For a long while, I felt lost without Johnny, and tried to keep in touch. But then Johnny left to live in America, and I found it difficult to forgive him for an act that Mother would have considered the supreme treachery. He did invite me to his wedding, and I could have gone, but chose not to. Other than one or two snippets of news sent by Father, I hadn't heard anything of Johnny till this commotion in the last couple of weeks.

I'd gone to visit Mother, and found her in the company of three men. One was an Australian Federal Police officer, and the other two were Americans, agents from the Federal Bureau of Investigation. One of the Americans was asking if she'd heard from Johnny, or if she knew of his whereabouts. They were surprised when she pointed to me.

Here's Johnny now. Why don't you ask him yourself?

The Americans are here to follow enquiries into a kidnapping. They believe that my brother Johnny has taken his two American children and brought them to Australia. I couldn't tell them whether this would be consistent with Johnny's recent behaviour. I did tell them that it was unlikely that Johnny would seek to make contact with either me or my mother.

Can you suggest where he might take the children? Is your brother a violent man? Would he be likely to harm them?

Though I was amused by the mention of violence in

connection with Johnny, I told the agents that I couldn't imagine Johnny being violent to his children. But harm was a different question.

How do you mean? the taller of the two Americans asked.

It's a matter of what you mean by harm, I said, making sure to look at my mother as I answered. If you asked Johnny, he'd tell you that he had the happiest childhood imaginable. If you told him that he meant to harm his kids, he'd tell you exactly what I'd tell you, that a few lousy haircuts and a diet of eggs never did anyone any harm.

A *letter to Francesca*

Three years ago, when I was a student at Melbourne University, my friend Catherine recommended to me the novel *Melbourne*, by the Brazilian writer, Julia Cortez. Though my main interest was in contemporary Australian fiction, I had previously read Cortez's collection of short stories, *Packing Death*. I found these stories to be rather affected and derivative, drawing heavily on the metaphysical ruminations of Borges and the so-called 'metafictive' games of recent American fiction. Still, I had no wish to question Catherine's judgement (I wanted to sleep with her), and the idea of a 'postmodern fantasy' set in the least fantastic of cities intrigued me.

I have since abandoned my PhD, and am now reading *Melbourne* for what must be the eleventh or twelfth time. The paperback that Catherine gave me disintegrated under the pressure of my pencilled notations. A second copy, in hardback, became so weighted with my notes that the text was unreadable. I now read from a hardback first edition, and make my notes in a series of Spirax notebooks. This most recent copy of *Melbourne* is inscribed by the author with the message: 'To Tim, the most diligent reader that any author could imagine, best wishes, Julia Cortez.' We correspond now, Julia and I.

My fascination with *Melbourne* began when I discovered that its central character and narrator, Richard Thompson, lives at 19 Passchendaele Street in the Melbourne suburb of Hampton, which happens to be my own address. When you read a detail like this in a novel, it takes some time to sink in. I can't imagine anything more curious than having a South American writer—who has, according to the publisher's blurb, never travelled outside her country—create a fictive character who lives at your address.

Naturally, I called Catherine, hoping that this coincidence might provide a good opportunity to test her affections.

Yes, I thought you'd be amazed, Catherine said. Julia Cortez is a wild writer. A lot of the coincidences are uncanny, don't you think? Like you and Richard for a start.

I've only read three pages so far, I said.

It gets better, believe me. But I don't want to ruin it for you. We should get together for a chat when you've finished.

That night I read the remaining 285 pages of *Melbourne*. A note on the title page of my paperback copy indicates that I finished reading at 4.40 am on the third of June, so I suppose that it must have taken five or six hours.

Looking back at it now, I can see that my earliest responses to the novel were neurotic, if not hysterical. Catherine must have thought that I would enjoy drawing parallels between myself and Richard. But I didn't enjoy the implications of those parallels.

I could only think that Catherine had set out to hurt me by recommending *Melbourne*, knowing it to be a novel that would tell me, specifically and unreservedly, that I am a lunatic. In my confusion I began to hate Catherine. I now regret the letter I wrote her the next day, not only because it became a police matter, but also because it foreclosed the opportunity for sexual engagement that may have become available. At the time I hated Julia Cortez also, for knowing so little, and presuming to know so much.

When I first read *Melbourne*, it seemed obvious that the author knew nothing about the city in which the novel is set. At least, nothing other than what Julia Cortez must have learnt from a street directory, probably *Melways*.

Most of the geographical references to suburban road and transport networks are accurate. The major public buildings, schools and parks are correctly named, but the information apparently deduced from the names is bizarre and often ridiculous.

In charting the progress of the number 8 tram down Toorak Road, for instance, Cortez's narrator, Richard, locates gasworks on the corner of Toorak Road and Chapel Street, which is the heart of Melbourne's most expensive shopping precinct. Early in the novel, Richard rides a train on the Sandringham line, but the vehicle is a double-decker train of the kind generally used in Sydney. While making this journey, Richard reflects somewhat harshly on the pollution he observes rising from factories in Brighton, which is, in reality, Melbourne's oldest establishment suburb, and free of such industries.

What I presumed to be errors and fabrications continued throughout Julia Cortez's novel. I began to compile a list headed 'Discrepancies and Variations in Julia Cortez's *Melbourne*'. The list fills 103 A4 pages, and notes, among many other things, climatic errors, errors in currency, perspective errors, gross historical errors, cultural misrepresentations, socio-economic errors, geopolitical misinformation, and the extreme unlikelihood that Richard's father would be distraught at having 'backed his Dodge over a wallaby when reversing from a driveway' in Hampton.

Had I simply posted this list to Julia Cortez via her Brazilian publishers, I might have saved myself a second major embarrassment. (I must say with regard to the first embarrassment that I had no intention of disembowelling Catherine, as my letter threatened, but it took some argument to persuade the magistrate of that.) Unfortunately, I included with the list a letter attacking Julia Cortez's characterization of Richard, and criticizing his erratic departures from reality.

Julia's reply (translated into English by Madeleine Elst, who translated *Melbourne* from the original Portuguese) is a model of patience and kindness.

August 17

Dear Tim,

Thank you for your letter and your interest in my novel *Melbourne*. Yours is certainly the most passionate response my fiction has yet provoked.

No Tim, you are not Richard Thompson. I did not imagine that my novel would be translated into English, so I did not anticipate that this problem might arise. I apologize for any embarrassment that may have been caused by abducting your address. I do not know any of your friends. No one has 'put me up to this', as you say.

Nor do I accept that Richard is mad. It seems to me that most of his behaviour is as sane as you could expect from a sensitive individual living in the quantum world. What happens to Richard may be internal, may be external, or may be allegorical. This is part of the amusement of fiction, don't you think? I choose to think of Richard as a 'post-romantic hero'.(Excuse the pun.)

I also beg to differ regarding your criticism of

19

Melbourne's 'copious errors'. On the contrary, the novel is a masterpiece of careful research, and I might suggest that I know more about the true city of Melbourne than many of its inhabitants. Where factual distortions and fabrications occur, they are indispensable to the mode of fiction I choose to call 'Theoretical Expressionism'.

Once more, thank you for your interest, Tim. Rest assured, I had no wish to depict you (or any real person) as a 'hyperbolically neurotic sociopath'.

Yours sincerely
Julia Cortez

The pun in this 'post-romantic hero' business has to do with Richard Thompson's obsessive letter-writing, which forms the core of *Melbourne*'s narrative.

Richard is a student of philosophy who lives at home with his parents in Hampton, just as I do. He finds it difficult to concentrate on his studies, distracted by the absence of his girlfriend, Francesca, who is travelling through Europe. Richard writes to Francesca daily. He has so little to write about that he begins to create fantastic tales of the city and the suburbs to amuse her. He invents plays and pop stars, sporting events and national heroes, impossible public buildings, and mysterious sightings of celebrities like Marlon Brando. Richard writes only about Melbourne, believing that his stories could only be appreciated by a like-minded Melburnian.

Francesca replies with humour and great enthusiasm. She encourages the game, and hints at the possibility of marriage when she returns. Then her correspondence stops.

Diplomatic enquiries reveal that Francesca has gone missing from a youth hostel on the outskirts of Copenhagen. As time passes, only Richard refuses to believe that she is dead. As a reader, I find it difficult to determine whether the situation has disturbed Richard's sense of reality, or whether an already disturbed sense of reality has been exacerbated by Richard's fears for Francesca. Richard re-reads Francesca's letters, over and over. He takes apart her letters word by word, believing that they must hold a clue to her disappearance. He continues to write to her, believing that one day Francesca will collect his letters.

After so many readings of *Melbourne*, I still fail to understand why Richard cannot accept the fact of Francesca's death. I will grant that he is smitten with Francesca, who has in her absence, become as important to his imaginative life as she had been to his lusts. But Richard is meant to be an intelligent, reflective man. I feel certain that I would be more fatalistic in the circumstances.

What could Richard hope to achieve by badgering authorities as he does? Foolishly, he rejects police advice and hires a Danish private detective, Andersen, an opportunist who sees the advantage in not reporting the obvious to Richard. Meanwhile, Richard persists in writing letters that (he must surely realize) betray a weak grasp on reality. Yet he remains capable of noting in his diary, 'I worry that I am a cerebral person who feels that he must pretend to this passion.'

Nearly a year ago I read a paper by a respected feminist critic who observed how frequently female characters go missing in Australian fiction. When their presence becomes too problematic or inconvenient for the (male) author, these women are murdered, or vanish, are transformed into leopards, or are revealed to be figments of the narrator's (mainly libidinous) imagination.

The same critic wrote that Julia Cortez's *Melbourne* ought to be read as an elaborate feminist critique of the vanishing woman in Australian fiction. Richard has rendered himself vulnerable by allowing Francesca to authorize or define his fantasy life. In order to reclaim control of his fantasies, Richard must kill her off and reinvent her.

When I look at the photograph of Julia Cortez on the back flap of the hardback edition of *Melbourne*, I don't see her as a woman with an agenda. Julia has soft, generous features, and seems about to explode into a broad smile. I imagine her to be someone who would giggle, girlishly and unashamedly, when something amused her. Julia's eyes are not the eyes of a revolutionary. Julia has the eyes of a storyteller.

As an author in the South American tradition, Julia Cortez has a multiplicity of intentions, but I do not see her as a political hardliner, nor am I aware of any evidence that would establish her acquaintance with recent Australian fiction. In my thoughts of Julia, I prefer to emphasize her mystery and complexity—her handwriting is like an art-work—and these qualities would be diminished were she to be cast as an ideologue.

When I place this first photograph next to the photo-graph of Julia Cortez on the back cover of the paperback edition, it strikes me that Julia does not look Brazilian. At least, she does not resemble the mental impression I have of a Brazilian. Julia Cortez looks to me like a northern Italian, a wonderfully stylish woman who would turn heads—male and female—as she walked the streets of Florence and Milan.

It has occurred to me that when Richard describes his beautiful Italian–Australian girlfriend, Francesca, I have been picturing a young woman who resembles the photo-graphs of Julia Cortez that appear on the various covers of *Melbourne*. 'No man or woman who has the opportunity to know you,' Richard writes to Francesca, 'could fail to fall at least a little bit in love with you.'

By picturing Francesca as Julia, I gain some knowledge of the anguish that prompts Richard to behave so irrationally. But how is the reader of *Melbourne* to explain Francesca's postcards?

Several months after Francesca's disappearance a postcard arrives in the mail, addressed to Richard, but unsigned. Though the postcard carries an Australian stamp, and a Melbourne postmark, the message appears to have been written by Francesca. At least, Richard is satisfied that the message has been written by Francesca. The message reads: 'R, meet me under the spires of the Castillo at 6 pm on my birthday.' The police are not convinced, believing it to be a cruel practical joke.

For the Melburnian reading *Melbourne*, the postcard is unusual in that it features the photograph of an ornate, Spanish–Gothic building known as the 'Castillo del Flinders'. A typed caption on the card describes the Castillo as 'Melbourne's most prominent late-eighteenth century building'. Given that most Australian readers of *Melbourne* would be aware that white settlement of Melbourne dates from the 1830s, the assertion of this fantastic building is disturbing. An earlier reference to the Castillo in one of Richard's letters to Francesca locates the building 'opposite the Treasury Gardens on the corner of Spring and Flinders Streets'. Richard, as we recall, has fabricated tales of a fantastic Melbourne to amuse Francesca, but it remains unclear to me as a reader of *Melbourne* whether the Castillo, 'notable for golden corkscrew spires which can be seen from distant suburbs of Melbourne', is part of a reality that Julia Cortez has fabricated for Richard, or one of Richard's own fabrications.

Richard waits at the appointed place at the appointed hour, but his Francesca does not arrive. Nor does anyone contact Richard claiming to be the author of the card.

The Castillo card is the first of a succession of bizarre postcards that arrive at Richard's home, each arranging an appointment that is never kept by the correspondent. Dismissing police opinions that the cards are a sadistic and ingenious hoax, Richard waits in parks, waits in restaurants, and waits under statues dedicated to the memory of historical figures whose names, deeds and existence make no sense to anyone who knows the real Melbourne.

Confused and desperate, Richard's narrative becomes painful to read. He begins to hate this Francesca who taunts him, and is tempted to suicide when he becomes ashamed of his own hostility.

Clearly, Julia Cortez invites the reader to balance the surmise of Richard's madness against the likelihood of a conspiracy, which may or may not involve Richard. Replying to one of my early letters, Julia dismissed the suggestion that enemies are conspiring against her narrator.

> Tim, you say that my novel is like Alfred Hitchcock's film *Vertigo*, full of spiralling confusions and conspiring minds. You suggest that someone may be trying to discredit Richard by getting him to assert the existence of an imaginary, resurrected Francesca. But you must remember that Richard is a no one. Who would want to discredit Richard? Richard is just a philosophy student who has scarcely been touched by the real world. He takes himself and his grief too seriously. *You* take him too seriously!

Like most authors, Julia plays down the significance of her own work. However, her novel *Melbourne* fascinates critics who are more eminent than I. The noted American scholar Allen Doust argues that Francesca never actually leaves Melbourne. Doust reads Francesca's 'European trip' as a fantastic, intimate game played out with her lover. (In their letters, she and Richard speak of 'Europe' as a kind of

Disneyworld, hypothesizing a network of very elaborate film stages constructed on the northern outskirts of Melbourne.) According to Doust, their letters, and her 'disappearance in Copenhagen', take place within the framework of complex erotic invention.

We should recognize that Allen Doust is a member of a critical school that sees all literature as a game, or mirror-maze. Even if Professor Doust was to read of Francesca's kidnapping in the morning edition of the *New York Times*, her plight would be little more than a literary game to him. No one has ever murdered the Professor's wife or girlfriend. Only someone who shares a Hampton address with Richard Thompson could appreciate the way that *Melbourne* connects with very real confusion and pain.

In her most recent letter, Julia continues to berate me and ridicule my theories, but I know that she does so because I am closing in on the truth, that I live in the emotional vicinity of the truth.

February 25th

Dear Tim,

I'm begging you to put down my novel and start with something new. Your personality is not suited to academic enquiry. When you first began to write to me, you described my novel as a 'psycho-critique' of your own life, suggesting that I was in league with your friend Catherine.

Now you acknowledge that you had it all wrong, telling me that *Melbourne* is 'a celebration; an incitement to a divided man standing at the threshold of a new life'. I would like you to retain this point of view, but you must dispense with the idea of 'prescription'.

Tim, *please understand*, I am not a kindred spirit prescribing a course of action for you (or your city, for that matter). You are confusing the fact that my novel is set at your address with the idea that it is addressed to you.

I am particularly disturbed by what you say about the need for Catherine to disappear and be reinvented. I am concerned for you, and I am concerned for Catherine. Catherine is not Francesca. She will not 'be made real by being reinvented'. Be sensible, Tim, and leave her alone.

I try not to tell people how to live, Tim. My novel touched you, but it does not seem to have enriched your understanding. I don't believe that you will ever find happiness by reading yourself into my novel. You may find peace by leaving Melbourne.

My most recent novel is due to be published this Friday. The narrative is set in San Francisco, and I expect that its title will translate as *Approximate Life*. I hope that you will read it and experience it (only) as a grand entertainment.

Yours sincerely
Julia Cortez

Of course, I had spoken of Catherine only by way of example, and Julia's overstated anxiety betrays her fear of my intuition. I can live without Catherine, just as I can live without plaudits from Julia, but I cannot leave *Melbourne* alone.

Richard is not a madman. He is not a no one. He has fervour and imagination. In fact, I am beginning to prefer Richard's Melbourne, with its gigantic edifices, to my own. If nothing else, Richard is loyal to his vision . . .

I trust that you will forgive the poverty of this tale, Francesca. Your continued silence dismays and unsettles me.

The Youth Hostel in Copenhagen has written asking me to send no more letters to their address. They say that they will return the letters that I have sent. Consequently, I will post this to your bank in London.

I long to hear from you, to kiss you again. Promise me that you will be in Melbourne for your birthday. We will drink champagne under the great golden spires.

My love, always, R.

Marlon Brando

Tell me what happened.

I was writing a short story. A kind of love story.

Yes?

Well, I'd got to the part where the hero, Tim, has a chance meeting with the girl of his dreams. Before he can appreciate the significance of the meeting, the girl is gone. Then he sees her in the distance and chases her. The girl is about to board a tram. Tim realizes that if he loses her now, she is lost forever. That's when it happens.

What happens? Tell me exactly what happens.

The girl, Catherine, is pushing through a crowd of people at the tram stop, and one of them turns out to be Marlon Brando.

Marlon Brando, the actor?

Yes.

At a tram stop in Melbourne?

Don't ask me what he's doing there, but it's definitely

Marlon Brando. He's just wandered into the crowd of people waiting at the tram stop.

And?

And? . . . This is Marlon Brando! Do you know what it costs to have Marlon Brando appear in one of your stories?

But it's an accident, surely?

Accident or not, it costs the same. If Marlon Brando wanders into the foreground of your story, you're up for one million dollars. If Marlon actually says something, stops to ask someone the time, you're talking another ten million, at least.

But you're The Author?

[Pause] Yes.

Can't you control what's going on?

[Silence]

It is a matter of control, isn't it?

Stories aren't like film sets. On film sets they have security controlling who comes and goes.

[Pause] *Tell me, are you a premature ejaculator?*

[Pause] Sometimes.

Often?

Sometimes.

You can see what I'm getting at, can't you?

[Silence]

Can't you just erase him?

He's there. He's part of the story now.

So what happens?

I could finish the story and sell it. If I sell the story, at best it will fetch me one hundred dollars. But it will cost me one million for having Marlon Brando in it. [Pause] What a bitch! Marlon Brando wanders into one of your stories, and your literary career is over.

That's bad luck.

Yes.

Couldn't you . . .?

What?

Couldn't you just . . .?

Couldn't I what?

Couldn't you just kill yourself?

[Pause] I wouldn't give Marlon the pleasure.

The Leisure Society

Klaus and Heiki had a really good time . . .

Klaus Obermeier has promised to buy me a new BMW and a three-bedroom apartment in Berlin if I continue to help him. Klaus insists that his project can't be finished without me. I feel sorry for Klaus. He's rich, but he's not a bad bloke, and his wife Heiki is the most tolerant person I've ever met. When the Obermeiers tell me that my help is crucial, I tell them that I appreciate their difficulties, and that I'd like to help, but I'm tired, and my dog is growing old. What's more, I'm beginning to suspect that Klaus is beyond assistance.

I'd never heard of Klaus Obermeier till four years ago. His brother Rudi moved into Passchendaele Street two or three years before that, and I often used to see Rudi with his three boys, kicking a soccer ball around the High School oval. I would give a slight nod as Rudi's family drove past in their sky-blue Mercedes. Other than that, I had nothing to do with them. Rudi's English was good, but Anna and the boys spoke little English then. Later, someone told me that Rudi had come to Melbourne to

manage the local subsidiary of Klaus' firm, Svekels, which
has its headquarters in Bremen.

Even in retirement, Klaus is one of Germany's best-
known industrialists. His company developed digital timing
mechanisms accurate to one millionth of a second, and sold
the technologies to space agencies around the world. By
the time he retired, Klaus had a personal fortune that made
him one of the wealthiest men in Europe. Not that you
would have guessed at that kind of family wealth from
Rudi and Anna's lifestyle. The local Obermeiers always
looked comfortable enough, and drove the best car in
Hampton, but they bought an unpretentious weatherboard
house, and sent their boys to state schools, though they
must have been able to afford the top shelf.

When Klaus retired at sixty, he was determined that he
and Heiki would enjoy themselves. They would be as
single-minded in their pursuit of pleasure as Klaus had
been in his mission to build Svekels. Heiki liked to collect
paintings, and Klaus was keen to indulge his passion for
bushwalking and photography. They already knew Europe,
Africa, and the Americas, so they were eager to investigate
Australia. As a devoted family man, Klaus looked forward
to catching up with his youngest brother, Rudi.

Men who spend their working lives dividing time into
millionths of a second tend not to be frivolous, so Rudi
drew up a ten-week itinerary for Klaus and Heiki that
organised their movements in fine detail. And Rudi was
surprised when his brother rejected this itinerary. During
their many telephone conversations, Rudi had often told
Klaus of his enthusiasm for the relaxed way of life in
Australia, and Klaus and Heiki had rather taken to the idea
of being swallowed up in a great leisure society.

So, though few of us knew it at the time, for several
weeks in 1990, Hampton played host to a rotund German

billionaire and his vibrant wife. Klaus and Heiki used Rudi's home in Passchendaele Street as a base between trips to the farthest corners of the continent. They snorkelled, they bushwalked, they climbed Uluru, they bought Australian paintings, they ate barramundi and kangaroo, they scoffed wine, they slept out under the stars, they sailed on Sydney Harbour, they went caving, they saw a football match at the Melbourne Cricket Ground, and they attended the opera. Though Klaus and Heiki met with many wealthy Australians, including a brief lunch with the Prime Minister, they enjoyed the company of ordinary people too.

They would have met few Australians more ordinary than the Passchendaele Street neighbours Rudi invited to a special farewell barbeque. I didn't know Rudi well enough to score an invitation, but friends who attended tell me that Heiki made fabulous cakes, and that Klaus drank like a fish when he wasn't taking photographs. The couple told everyone that they'd had the trip of a lifetime, and that Klaus would have retired five years earlier if he'd known how much fun it was to live so hedonistically.

Maybe that feeling of elation would have worn off soon enough, I don't know. Klaus hugged strangers that he met at the barbeque. He told his brother that he was reluctant to leave. He even enthused about quiet, mundane Hampton. As he flew back to Germany, Klaus called his brother from every airport stopover to thank him for organising such a perfect holiday.

. . . but when they got back to Bremen, something terrible happened . . .

Klaus and Heiki could not stop telling their German family

and friends what a fabulous time they'd had staying with Rudi and travelling through Australia.

Wait till I show you the picture of the crocodile. You won't believe the size of it, he'd say.

The blue of the sky. The intense colours. You wouldn't credit the reds and blues in the centre of Australia, Heiki said.

The striped fish on the Barrier Reef.

Yes, the Barrier Reef was extraordinary, Heiki agreed.

We can't imagine how things could have been better. Everything worked out so perfectly.

Klaus sent seventeen rolls of colour film to be developed. No photographs were ever returned.

We're terribly sorry, Mr Obermeier, the manager told the billionaire. We simply can't account for your film.

Klaus was devastated. He reminded the film development company that he wasn't accustomed to sloppiness, and that he wouldn't be prepared to accept their sloppiness. He initiated legal actions. He threatened them with corporate takeover. But, despite the pressure Klaus applied to the company, nothing turned up. Seventeen rolls of film had vanished. Four hundred and eight lovingly composed shots taken with the most sophisticated photographic equipment available. Though Heiki could still admire the superb intricacy of her Aboriginal paintings, the swirling blues of her three Brett Whiteleys, and the weird sense of space in her massive Fred Williams, Klaus felt that his greatest moments had been taken from him.

He took out his notebook, and reminded Heiki of the unique brilliance of every one of the 408 photographs he had taken. The strange people. The peculiar shifting light at Katajuta. The magnificent dynamism of the footballers. Klaus swung between teary nostalgia and impotent fury.

Don't fret. There's nothing to stop us from going again, Heiki said.

You're damn right we'll be going again, Klaus told her.

. . . and the horror of his loss sent Klaus on a voyage in search of authentic moments

The fourteenth image on Klaus' sixteenth roll of film was a lucky shot by comparison with some of the more artful moments that he'd captured during his travels.

Rudi had been kicking the soccer ball with his fifteen-year-old son on the Hampton High School oval. Klaus liked their total absorption in the game, but, more particularly, he liked the quality of the late afternoon light. Dark stormclouds had gathered over the buildings to the east, sharply contrasting the red-gold brilliance in the west. The grass had turned pinky-green, the tall gums skirting the oval seemed to flame, and the two players cast long, mysterious shadows. It was one of those moments when you wish you had a camera with you, and Klaus always had his camera with him.

That's when I came into the picture.

I'd been running my cocker spaniel across the bottom end of the oval. I tossed a tennis ball, and Tuddy raced after it, leaping to catch it on the bounce. I nodded to Rudi and Michael, but I wasn't aware that Klaus was watching us, or that my dog and I had made ourselves an essential ingredient in one of the most perfect compositions Klaus had ever witnessed.

I doubt that I would have become aware of my part in Klaus's perfect moment if Klaus and Heiki hadn't returned to Australia determined to re-create every one of the 408 photographs that Klaus had lost.

To begin with, Klaus contented himself with rough approximations. One blue-gold fish swimming above a pink stretch of coral was as good as another. He wasn't concerned that Heiki should wear the same dress in the same location, so long as the dress was similarly coloured, that she occupied the same position, and took a roughly similar attitude. But Klaus is a serious photographer, and he wasn't prepared to compromise with the light.

He spent four weeks waiting for a sunset in Broome to match the sunset he photographed on his first night there. Never mind that he witnessed many more spectacular sunsets during his return stay, it had to be the same sunset. No bunch of footballers would do. They had to be the same three footballers, in a similar relation to each other, in a real game at the same venue. If just one of the three had been injured, or retired, Klaus would have spent a vast sum to extend his career. He would have paid-off team selectors, just for the sake of a single photograph.

Klaus told people that he'd never known the relaxation, or loss of inhibition that he had experienced in those two perfect months in Australia, and he wasn't going to accept the loss of his images or their associations. A memory wasn't enough. If the Leaning Tower of Pisa collapsed, it would have to be rebuilt exactly. It would have to be rebuilt with exactly the same propensity for collapse. And the idea of distortion horrifies Klaus. He is ruthless in his pursuit of authentically re-created perfections.

Somewhere along the line, Heiki lost interest. Everything went flat for her. She wanted to see new galleries, explore different areas, and do new things. Much as she understood her husband and his peculiar earnestness, she found it hard to come at visiting the same restaurants, with the same people, all ordering the same meals, just for the sake of a photograph that seemed banal in the first instance. She hated waiting for it to start raining. And she hated being embarrassed.

When the Prime Minister told Klaus that he was too busy to meet him for the purpose of re-staging a photograph, Klaus threatened to exercise his influence on the Svekels' board. Klaus could persuade the company to withdraw its subsidiary operation in Melbourne. Faced with the loss of a thousand jobs in a marginal electorate, the Prime Minister reconsidered. He didn't hesitate to send an aid on a four-hour round trip to fetch the tie that he'd worn on the occasion of his luncheon with Klaus.

Everything about this exercise has been a misery for Klaus, but he won't relent. When he first offered to pay me to walk my dog on the school oval at sunset, I told him that I didn't want to be paid. I figured that it wasn't such a big deal if it kept an important international visitor happy.

That was eighteen months ago. When I told Klaus that I would be unavailable to walk my dog at sunset *every* evening, he offered to pay me two hundred dollars a day. I would have refused, if Klaus hadn't already been sly enough to 'discuss matters' with my employer. Having spoken with Klaus, my employer revised my contract to ensure that work wouldn't get in the way of my availability to model for wealthy Germans.

But it isn't just me being fickle. My dog Tuddy has grown old. He has arthritis in his back legs, and he finds it hard to jump. In recent months, Tuddy has lost interest in chasing tennis balls.

I run in front of Tuddy clicking my fingers.

If you can't coax him, threaten him! Klaus shouts.

Klaus' nephew Michael is now a young man engaged in his final year of secondary study, and he would prefer not to spend long hours playing soccer with his father, but he does so under threat of disinheritance. It's even harder for his father. Rudi had a small heart-attack last year, and he really shouldn't be chasing after soccer balls every evening.

The real problem is the light, waiting for those same unique stormclouds. None of us will be real till we exist in a photographic image that corresponds to the reality in Klaus' memory, and we will only be authentic when we are authentic in a photograph that re-captures the authenticity of a moment when we were truly authentic. The longer this process takes, the less likely it is that this authentic moment will be successfully re-staged.

I want to help Klaus, because I know that he is feeling a loss that is beyond my understanding. And I feel sorry for Heiki. She wants to go home, and I'm certain that when she's at home in Bremen, she will refuse to view Klaus' 408 photographs. But the more we wait, and the more I try to help, the more I begin to suspect that Klaus has stirred something in me that won't go when he goes.

I have accepted Klaus' word that I was once accidentally part of a perfect moment, a moment that I have no memory of. And if I am so oblivious to real perfection, is there any use for me in life other than to be paid background for billionaires who wish to substantiate their authenticity?

I fear that one day I might discover that my only purpose was to exist for a single moment in which the accident of my existence lent substance to the life of someone I neither knew nor cared for. I might find that I had no importance besides a single moment stolen from time, to be lost forever by a German photographic company.

ickly heat

1 The Men with the Nets

Every public servant has a slightly different version of the same dream. They will be working in a vast office, full of desks, and filing cabinets, and computer terminals. The clerks seem edgy, consternated. They sense that something is about to happen. Someone drops a stack of files, or spills a cup of coffee. For some reason, the phones have stopped ringing. Filing clerks dart backwards and forwards, unable to concentrate on their immediate task. Normally silent officials chatter nervously.

Suddenly, the glass door which leads to the lift-wells is flung open, and a superior dashes into the room, bellowing, They're coming! Take cover!

Intuitively, we know who he means. We've been waiting for them without knowing that we've been waiting for them. The younger staff clamber up the filing cabinets, while senior officers take refuge under their desks, or in the toilets. Then they appear, tall men decked out in SWAT-style polo-necked jumpers, and peaked caps. Powerfully strong, agile men with dark moustaches. They move in slow motion. Even their speech sounds distorted, slowed down. Get that one! Get her! Two of them set after a young woman, and corner her as she scurries into a dead end. She shrieks, No! No! as the net drops over her.

Other men go searching down the aisles between tall filing cabinets, net in hand. A terrified clerk dashes across the centre of the office, and two men with a net begin to pursue him, before a superior shouts, Leave him! We only want the talented ones!

When two or three public servants have been collected in their nets, the invaders leave, to go about their business in offices elsewhere. No one tries to rescue the abducted officers. The incident is never spoken about. Soon, the office will be working as if nothing has happened.

Every public servant has a different version of a dream where the men with nets rush into their office, seize the talented people who ought not to be there, and take them to a place where their talents will finally be put to good use. As a public servant, you consider yourself to be living in temporary exile from your true destiny. One day, you will be snatched from your too-safe world and dragged screaming into the spotlight that's always awaited you.

2 Prickly Heat

Sleep is everything, the central preoccupation of the shift worker. Your head turns on the pillow, you feel the beam of warm sunlight hit your face, and you try not to think, not even about shifting the curtains, because thinking will take you further from sleep. But what you're thinking is that you'll be totally fucked at work if you can't get sleep. You know that terrible sick-in-the-gut, tongue-dead feeling of sleep deprivation. Telling yourself, you *must* get sleep, as if sleep, having slept, is something that you can hold on to.

It's the caffeine paradox. Because you haven't slept, you belt back coffee to get you through a night at the office, and now you can't sleep because of the caffeine dancing through your bloodstream. You try to piss it away, to piss it all out of your system, but always you're left with that insistent prickly sensation, like an army of tiny spiders racing across your skin. Two teams of prickle-footed spiders playing soccer on your skin. You can't rub them away. You can't piss them away. And before you know it, your eyes are wide open to the glare of the afternoon sun, thinking, Christ, what am I doing this for? Please, I'll do anything, just let me sleep.

And this, the caffeine poisoning, the spiders and the prickly-heated despair, is your punishment for murdering a Scottish King, for returning to the public service when you promised yourself that you'd starve rather than work another lousy office job. You'll have to say it out loud, because otherwise you're in danger of not believing it: You say, I'm better than this.

3 Godzilla versus the Manual Index

The Criminal Records section of the Police Department occupies one complete floor of a tall city office building. This building also houses the Fingerprint Division, the Missing Persons Office, the Fraud Squad, the Armed Robbers, Homicide, and Sexual Offences, along with an ordinary police station, and a Criminal Intelligence Branch.

If there is one experience shared by the civilian clerks and uniformed police working in the Records section, it is that they have all, at some time, stood in front of a mirror and thought, I deserve better than this.

The police are elderly sergeants on the verge of retirement, or young sergeants and senior constables using the office as a stepping stone to seniority. The poorly paid clerical officers are students taking a break between studies, kids working their first job, or the tragedy cases at a port of last resort, all desperately hoping that something better will turn up.

You are one of the tragedies. After teacher training, you'd decided that you didn't have the right stuff to teach unshaven fourteen year olds, and now you tell yourself that you only need to work at Criminal Records while you await the outcome of two job applications, the first to be an English teacher in Japan, the second to be a student at the National Film School in Sydney. Though you have worked in several government offices, this is a Siberia like no other.

Because crime never takes a holiday, the phones never stop ringing. Criminal records checks. Security checks. Shooter's licence checks. Warrant checks. In order to serve officers on the beat, the section stays open twenty-four hours a day, and clerks are rostered on in three eight-hour shifts. After a time, the job begins to take hold of your body. When you aren't sleeping, or thinking of sleep, you are on the phone, or up to your wrists in the file cards that make up the near-infinite manual index of Victorians boasting a criminal record. Names, false names, and nicknames, millions of file cards jammed tight into the narrow draws of grey cabinets that circle a vast room. Persons frequently known to police have their records made up into comprehensive files known as dockets. Each year, four or five thousand new dockets are added to the collection.

You are engulfed by ignobility. This is the shadow history of Melbourne and Victoria. Halfway through a tough shift you get lost in all those cards and files so that your head spins with names and tattoos, the dates and codes and protocols and prohibitions, the half-remembered list of corrupt officers who aren't to be given information, and the officers whose names are to be recorded if too much interest is shown in sensitive information. Juvenile criminals, druggies, Old School criminals, careerists and psychopaths, you live with them night and day.

There is a complete cabinet full of cards—thousands of cards—detailing criminals known to have tattoos on their penis.

One young prostitute has a cat and a mousetrap tattooed on her left inner thigh, a mouse and **SOME CHEESE** on her right inner thigh, and a dog under her left breast. She is gradually transforming her body into a relief map of the food chain.

A tall, flame-headed member of a bike gang has just one tattoo which takes up his entire chest: Donald Duck smoking an enormous joint while sodomizing Mickey Mouse, accompanied by the speech balloon, 'It's grouse if you can get it'.

On the phone, you inform officers of priors and pendings, suspicions and outstanding warrants, the persons to be approached with caution, and the premises believed to house stashes of weapons. Always the swirl of names and birthdates and spellings, possible spellings, and alternative spellings, till you find yourself riffling through the manual index at four in the morning, having lost all confidence in your ability to order the letters of the alphabet. You live in fear that a new letter may have been added to the alphabet since your last shift.

This index of criminals infiltrates your consciousness. To your friends outside work you can talk about nothing but crime and criminals. And you can never get over how much recorded crime there is. You try to persuade yourself that it's natural that a city of three million should have crime, but not this much crime surely. This much brutality and deception and indecency.

The Homicide detectives want information urgently. The police on the road want information now. If you fuck up, if you flick over one index card in a tray of thousands, if you fail to consider an alternative spelling, or the possibility that two similarly named criminals may be one and the same, a superior will arrive to tear you to shreds. If you miss one crucial thread of information, someone might die. And all the time, you are sleepless, or else your sleep is polluted with images of the vast Manual Index.

When the interview for the teaching position in Japan finally comes up, you haven't slept for seventy-two hours. You sit opposite a panel of two Australian women and a Japanese man. Even the most predictable question no longer has an obvious answer. Why do you want to teach in Japan? You riffle through your mind, but your mind is stuffed full of the names of criminals, and the physical descriptions of criminals.

Why do I want to teach in Japan? Getting desperate now. Why *do* I want to go to Japan? They are waiting for your answer. Think! *Think!*

Your desperate answer, that you'd like to meet Godzilla, does not convince the Japanese Government to offer you a teaching position.

The Manual Index may yet prove to be your destiny.

4 The Unknown Criminal

A new filing cabinet is requested to accommodate the constantly expanding Manual Index. When the Stores

Branch stuff up the order, two cabinets are delivered, the second standing empty next to the cabinet jammed thick with W to Z miscreants. After a time, one of the staff tapes an identikit photo of a criminal to the drawers of the empty cabinet, along with the label, 'Tomb of the Unknown Criminal'.

It isn't such a big joke, and the photograph and label would have been removed soon enough if local detectives hadn't warmed to the idea. Detectives from the Homicide Squad, and the Sexual Offences Squad began to stand before the Tomb of the Unknown Criminal, hoping for a moment of inspiration as they continued their investigation into an unsolved crime. Superstition soon becomes tradition among the superstitious. Within a matter of weeks, no one even thought to question the idea of a detective pausing head-bowed in front of an empty filing cabinet.

5 Distractions

There are quiet times. The cold, wet mornings when even the hardest criminals prefer bed. As soon as the phones stop ringing, we start organizing our competitions, and gather nominations for the Mongrel of the Month Award. Each month, the criminal who perpetrates the worst crime or crimes takes out The Mongrel, and remains in the running for nomination to the Hall of Shame. The Hall receives three new inductees each December. Hall of Shamers are mongrels *par excellence*. You are sure that they would be proud of the honour if they could be notified. Our oath of confidentiality prevents us from informing recipients of their new status. Nevertheless, we write induction speeches on their behalf, and deliver them in their absence. The speeches are always polite and grateful.

Parents are thanked. Family and schoolteachers. Society at large. Invariably, the new Hall of Shamers promise not to let the honour distract them from their mission. They will remain dedicated to a life of malevolence.

6 The Line-up

One morning a supervisor calls together the young male clerks. We are asked to go downstairs to the Victims of Crime section to take part in a line-up. Though it isn't irregular for office staff to make up numbers for a line-up, this is your first time. As a film buff, you imagine that the whole thing will be like Hollywood film noir. In Hollywood movies, the victim stands anonymous behind double-plated glass as a line-up of suspects is paraded under an intense lamp. This arrangement is designed to protect the victim from retribution or threats.

But that's Hollywood. Maybe that arrangement doesn't exist anywhere in reality. When we arrive downstairs, we are taken into a large auditorium. Twenty men have been invited from different sections of the building. A detective asks us to form a line at one end of the room. We are told to remove our police ID tags. You presume that their suspect is the thin, blond man who doesn't have a tag to remove.

Then a woman is escorted into the rear of the room by two detectives. She is a petite brunette. Pretty. She smokes a cigarette. Even from a distance, you can see the cigarette tremble in her fingers.

The woman is brought to the front of the auditorium to stand no more than two or three metres from the line of men. She stands there, smoking, looking down at her feet, while one of the detectives reads out details of the circumstances in which the woman was raped.

As she walked along a street at night, she was dragged off the footpath into the back seat of a parked car, where she was violently assaulted. The detective says that unlawful sexual penetration is alleged to have taken place. While he reads, the woman smokes and looks down. There are twenty men listening to the details of the offence against her. She is the only woman in the room.

Then one of the detectives asks the woman whether her assailant is one of the men standing in the line-up. The woman looks closely at the first seven or eight men standing in the line before taking a very cursory scan of the men further down the line. You don't remember if she ever looked directly into your face. You doubt that she looks down the line as far as the thin, blond man you presume to be the suspect.

The detective asks her again, formally, whether her assailant is in the line-up. The woman says, No.

After the woman has been escorted from the room, we are told that we can go back to our sections. A detective thanks us for our participation.

As you go upstairs to the phones and the Manual Index, you think about the meaning of the verb to participate, and decide that you have participated. You had participated by allowing the detective to thank you for participating. And already your participation has left you feeling strangely unclean.

7 *The Shades of Criminality*

The year gets worse for you. The National Film School advise that they cannot offer a place in their one-year screenwriting course, and now your only hope of acceptance is to gain admission into the school's three-year Bachelor of Arts course. To succeed, you will need to be one of the anointed twelve from a field of seven hundred applicants nationwide. You have written just one short script, and you have never even looked through a video camera. The worry makes you look at your clerical colleagues, and wonder whether, forty years from now, you will die with them at your side, surrounded by an ever vaster, ever dustier labyrinth of files, index cards, and cabinets.

During meal breaks, you talk about old hit records and television shows. One cartoon that often comes to mind is 'Tooter and The Wizard' from *Leonardo The Lion*.

Tooter was a kid who always thought that the grass would be greener in another place at another time, and the kindly old wizard, a very Viennese Freud caricature, assisted by transporting Tooter through time to the historical moment of his choice. Invariably, Tooter got himself into strife, being attacked by pirates and Indians and communists, and when things were at their most desperate, Tooter would fall to his knees and bellow, Mr Wizard! Mr Wizard! At which the know-it-all wizard waved his wand and incanted, Teetle, tattle, tootle, tum, time for this one to come home, so relieving Tooter from the misery of spatio-temporal dislocation.

There are times when every public servant would like to fall to his or her knees and scream, Mr Wizard! Mr Wizard!

This is a record breaking year. There are twenty-five murders in six weeks, even before the massacre at Hoddle Street, where a demented army reject shoots motorists as they drive home late on a Sunday night. Several days later, there is a particularly brutal double-murder in

Sandringham, and you find yourself sharing a lift with two Homicide detectives. They talk casually about the football, and why Essendon has had such a poor season. One of them holds a sealed plastic bag which contains a blood-stained kitchen knife.

Murder seems to be closing in on you. You remind yourself that exile in the public service is your punishment for murdering a Scottish King, for not heeding the voice of reason. It may be that you will catch this murder virus.

8 Rare Passion

A police officer in Moorabbin calls to enquire about the record of a suspect, formerly resident in Western Australia. A telex is sent to the Criminal Records Office in Perth, and after twenty minutes you are able to inform the requesting officer that his suspect has a prior conviction for 'Attempted Carnal Knowledge of a Horse'.

This the first time you've seen the offence referred to in this way. More commonly, it would be 'Gross Indecency', or 'Aggravated Cruelty to an Animal', or even, in some statutes, 'Bestiality'. Still, the sergeant takes it in his stride. You overhear him speaking to the suspect.

Had a bit of trouble with a horse out west, did we, mate? Never mind, he tells the offender, I know how it is. You're in the darkness of a crowded disco, and someone special takes your fancy. She may be fifteen. She may be sixteen. When a bloke's in the throes of a rare passion, he's not going to stop to count her teeth.

9 The Persistence of Memory

You have two conflicting desires, to sleep, and to drink

coffee, and these desires are locked in mortal combat. However much you beg for sleep, it eludes you. Coffee, on the other hand, is always there when you need it, and you always need it.

A woman sits opposite you in a South Yarra cafe one lunchtime as you stop for a coffee on the way to an afternoon shift. Though you seem to remember her face, you can't place her. The longer you look at her, the more you are convinced that she is someone you know. You could approach her and ask, Don't I know you?, but you hate to use lines that sound so much like lines.

The woman is small and dark-haired, probably in her early thirties. She is pretty enough to be someone you might have seen on television, or in a magazine. Equally, she could be someone you worked with in the past. Mostly, you remember things, but lately you've been finding it difficult to situate your memories.

For just an instant, she makes eye contact. She realizes that you've been looking at her, and shifts her gaze. She gulps down the last of her coffee, and fumbles through her purse to find coins to cover the bill.

You are sure that you know her from somewhere. You watch her hurry out of the cafe. She is half a block down Toorak Road before you realize that she is the woman who once examined your face while you stood in a police line-up.

10 The Fuck-up

It's nearly December, and you've heard nothing from the Film School. There has been another insane massacre. This time a gunman has gone on the rampage in the centre of Melbourne, terrorizing an office building in Queen

Street. You're so twitchy that the slightest contact with another human being makes you jump.

It's Friday afternoon, and you're re-filing index cards when a highly agitated detective slams open the swinging door that leads to the Manual Index. From behind a cabinet, you hear him yelling at one of your superiors. It's obvious that there's been a fuck-up. All the clerks fall silent, and wait to see who is going to be scapegoated. The detective and the supervisor riffle through the inquiry sheets to see which clerk handled the record request in question. After a time, you see the two of them striding in your direction.

You! the detective shouts. Did I speak to you on the phone about a crim named Cook?

You remember that you checked the files for a Cook earlier that afternoon. The detective is red in the face.

You told me that Alastair Cook wasn't recorded or wanted, didn't you? Then how the fuck is it that this Alastair Cook did time for grievous bodily harm? How come he's got an apprehension warrant outstanding for escape and attempted murder?

You look at the sheets, and the index card in front of you, and try to work out what happened, but the detective is prodding you in the chest with his index finger. Jabbing the place between your chest and your shoulder-blade. Jabbing hard enough to push you back against a filing cabinet. The supervisor tries to grab his arm, but he keeps jabbing you hard.

We had Cook, but because you're a lazy fuckwit, we let him go.

Your colleagues have put down their phones so that they can circle your humiliation, so that they can see you get punished for the fuck-up.

You are trying to explain that Cook's Christian name had

been spelled out to you as Alistair, and that the Alistair Cooks and the Alastair Cooks ought to have been consolidated in the index, but in fact there were twenty Albert Cooks and Alfred Cooks separating Alistair from Alastair. You want to tell the detective that it's not your fault, that it's the fault of this impossible Manual Index. You want to say that there are bound to be errors when clerks are filing and re-filing millions of error-laden index cards. You'd say all this, but the detective is hitting you in the chest with his fist.

I'm not getting through to you, am I? A member might have got killed because you failed to warn him that he was dealing with a fiend. And this head is still out on the fucking street. He might kill someone yet.

You want to fall on your knees and beg. You want to scream out, Mr Wizard! Mr Wizard! But you know that cartoon wizards can't save you from real-life injustice. The detective is punching you, and your colleagues are watching him punch you, too fearful to intervene. You are crying.

Then, just as the detective seems ready to reorganize your face, someone picks him up, and heaves him onto the table in the middle of the room. You see the other staff scatter. You see a net descending over your head, and hear a slow, distorted voice pronounce, That's the one! Take him!

You are being carried away by two men at either end of a large black net.

Your colleagues are stunned when they see that no one else is to be taken. They run to protest. They try to tell the men with the net that you're not talented, that you're not entitled to be rescued. They say that only just now you've caused a major fuck-up.

We're much more talented than him, they say. Take us!

But everything is in motion now. You've never felt so

comfortable and safe as you feel embraced by that net. You feel your skin beginning to relax. You feel the calm certainty of approaching sleep. You know that when you wake, you'll be five hundred miles away from the Manual Index, a student at the National Film School in Sydney.

And much later, when you're safely making student films, when you've nearly forgotten the constant prickling sensation of caffeine overdose, you just might kid yourself that you live in a world where everyone gets their just desserts, and that this is the only way that your story could have turned out.

Time and motion

1

I will begin where she likes it best. My hand poised palm down, not more than a few centimetres above her naked breast. Movement is forbidden. She is not to be distracted by even a spider of shadow advancing toward her neck. Two minutes, fifteen seconds.

Only a trained eye would perceive any transformation. Tracey's glazed eyes make her appear to be under hypnosis. Four minutes, twenty-three seconds. She drags in a single breath, kicks once, twice, involuntarily, exhales hard. It's over.

I admit that I don't fully understand this fashion of lovemaking, just what the tantalizing hand represents, nor the role it plays in the construction of her fantasy. But her pleasure is evident, indubitable. Tracey will tell me that we are exploring the economics of love, and that together we shall lay the foundations for a model economy.

She will throw on a short black kimono and make an entry on her chart. My time and motion woman.

from 'An Interim Report on
Our Failure to Achieve Maximum
Effective Utilization of Finite Sexual
Vitality'

Tracey notes that of 413 occasions I have declared my love
to her, 118 would have sufficed to achieve the same ends.

That I tend to lick anything and everything, running
short of stamina at crucial moments.

That I have an unfortunate clockwise bias in all circular
motions.

That I came prematurely on no less than 76 occasions
in her initial two-year study, and that 57 of these unsolicited
spurts contravened specific instruction.

She notes that I 'buggerize around being romantic' when
sexual initiative is required, and ignore romance as soon as
I have purchased an erection.

That despite being significantly more effective on the
kitchen table and the dining room floor (52%), I show a
selfish preference for the bedroom (24%).

That I was actually incapable of achieving penetration
on 27 occasions; 21 times at night, 6 times in the morning.

She notes that I am sometimes (3%) guilty of foreplay
that is effectively counter-productive.

That I concentrate too much upon the erotic, and too
little on the aerobic.

That my concentration wanders.

That the flabbiness of my buttocks suggests a loss of
focus, and insufficient preparation.

She notes that no less than 9% of my advances were
insincere.

3

On a bad day, it occurred to me that I might not be the only participant in Tracey's study. I had been shocked to read some graffiti on a toilet door at the university, 'Together we approximate exactitude'. It's a maxim of Tracey's. What she means by it, I'm not quite sure, but that isn't the point. Why was her maxim written in texta on a door in the men's toilets?

Perhaps foolishly, I have assumed that her study is without limit, ongoing. I considered that we, she and I, were the point of the study. Yet just now she might be approximating exactitude with any of a host of participant subjects. Well, not just now.

Now, Tracey is turning the bend in Swanston Street. It will take her twenty seconds to walk past the City Baths. Being hot, she will cross to the brewery side to be in the shade. Two minutes up the hill, maybe faster if she thinks that someone is eyeing her off. Time, she's told me on more than one occasion, is synonymous with accountability. How can there be others? Tracey's autobiography would read like a street directory, only more organized.

I mustn't underestimate her. It may be that Tracey's study has a point of termination. She might simply collect her logs, journals and stop-watches, and undertake to approximate exactitude with another or others.

No, it's unthinkable.

It's unthinkable that she could abandon any task short of perfection. And perfection isn't a signpost that we've located all that often. When it's perfect, she insists, the word fuck will be onomatopoeic. Our lovemaking will find substance in efficiency, a poetic in the economic.

4

Tracey took the keys for the Datsun. I heard her back out of the driveway and ease off down the hill. She drives as methodically as she eats, as she speaks, as she makes love.

If it weren't for her method, her precise algebraic reasoning, I might have felt guilty riffling through the drawers and filing cabinets in her study. It's an unethical way to carry on, but it can't be less than what she expects of me. Much as Tracey wants me to be an economist, the clinical analyst of specific relations and conditions, she knows that at heart I am an explorer obsessed with the erotic aspects of personality.

I couldn't be certain that Tracey kept a personal diary, no more than the Dutch or Portuguese could be certain of the existence of a Terra Australis. Nevertheless, it was a surmise that had formed the basis of my faith.

Should I call it that, faith?

No, not faith. Maybe I was expecting that in her secret moments, in her time outs from timekeeping, she would detest me. I might uncover her true disdain for my cowardice, for the pathetic self-consciousness that descends into self-obsession. Anything. I became ruthless, tossing aside reams of print-outs, her manila folders bulging with column upon column of statistical data, the rulers and liquid paper, until there it was. Her personal journal.

I had made a list of crucial dates and events, so that I could discover exactly what she had been thinking when her thoughts mattered most to me. Had I made even the slightest impression on her hidden realm of emotion? These hopes of mine were so foolish. They failed to take account of Tracey's ability to double-guess my movements, to lure me toward an anticipated destination. Inside the journal, I found just one entry, written in a hand that was unmistakable.

> *Tracey*
> She
> who infuriates, incarcerates,
> evaporates, and threatens
> to disappear
> without Trace,
> who reflects a shadow
> extended beyond time, beyond fate,
> who begins and ends
> always and utterly
> in the spider realm of my desire.
> My time and motion woman.

I closed the journal. Was I to believe that she had made herself absent to effect my annihilation? Or was it that we were moving even closer to the signposts that Tracey had chosen? Perfection. Exactitude.

5

2.30 Tracey addresses her class. She cleverly modulates her deep voice to achieve proper emphasis. Though many of these students will lust after her, will they really see her? Will they notice that she implies absence, or that I have her measure and pass through her at will? They could hardly be expected to understand that she is my complement, and that her need for me, her need to have her measurements ratified, taunts her. I tantalize her.

5.30 Her car in the driveway. Her briefcase in the hall. Tracey will remove her blouse and take position beneath the shadow of my palm. Then we will begin again in the way she likes best.

Motion sickness

Leaving Central Station the train travels in reverse for fifty minutes until it arrives at a Y-junction on the outer perimeter of the city. Many new travellers are disturbed by this unexpected reverse motion and try to swap seats so that they can travel forwards. Being accustomed to the peculiarities of the journey, I explain to confused passengers that the train will assume their favoured direction as soon as it leaves the suburbs.

As it happens, I prefer reverse motion when I travel. You can watch the suburbs peel away like cellophane packaging, and can imagine that they feature in a film being screened incorrectly. You expect that a point will arrive when the screen will go to black. Then, after a frenzy of activity in the projection room, the film will be rescreened as its director intended. Travelling backwards enables me to imagine that everything done might be undone.

The man who sat opposite was in his early-twenties, red-headed, a little scruffy, probably a student. He wanted to get the attention of the pretty brunette sitting next to me. At first, the girl seemed indifferent to his vacuous chat, and refused to give him eye contact. Then he realized, at about the same time that I did, that the young woman was deaf. After that, we all communicated in a pigeon sign language that had the young woman in hysterics. Her exuberant smile reminded me of Christine, a girl that I was fond of before I married. (I cannot go anywhere without seeing these resemblances.) My neighbour's speech was a monotonous mish-mash of sound, frequently impenetrable, but from what we could make sense of, she was a well-educated person who worked as an animator for a foreign company.

I had mistaken the man's first approaches to be a brazen play for the young woman's affections. As it transpired, his sole aim had been to share his joy with anyone who cared to listen.

Only the previous evening, the man had become engaged to his first cousin, an arrangement that had been postponed for several years owing to the disapproval of a mutual grandparent, now deceased. The young man was on his way to tidy up some business, then the two cousins would marry as soon as he returned.

Alice is extraordinary, the man said. We knew that we would marry from the very first, from when we used to play together as kids.

From his wallet the man produced a snapshot of himself standing alongside a radiant, red-headed girl. My neighbour commented that the man's fiancée was very pretty, which was undeniable. With the man so unrestrained in his delight, I felt that it would be imprudent to say that I could detect a strong family resemblance.

We each drank from the man's large bottle of vodka, and the three of us continued to giggle over the imprecision of our signed gestures, joking a little bawdily as the train rumbled into the evening-pink countryside. The alcohol accentuated my tiredness, and I fell into a deep sleep not long after the compartment lights went down at eleven.

That night I dreamt of something that may have taken place when I was eleven or twelve. I say may have taken place, because it is unclear to me at this distance whether the incidents I remember relate to an actual event, or to an unusually vivid dream that I had at that time. My father was taking me by train into the city to buy my first adult cricket bat. As no one in our family owned a car, we rarely left our suburb, and the city seemed to me to be a confusion of dark laneways and backstreets. I was thankful that my father knew the way.

At the sporting goods store, my father agreed to stretch his budget so that I could buy the brand of bat endorsed by my idol. The old salesman smiled with stained yellow teeth as I caressed the smooth willow face of the blade with my open hand. He advised my father that I should purchase a bottle of linseed oil, instructing me how and when I should apply the oil.

I was remarkably happy to have the full attention of my father, and to be the owner of a new bat. But, as the train neared our station on the return journey, I realized that the bumping motion of the old red carriage had given me a very conspicuous erection. I became worried that my father would notice, that he would think that I was shameless, and I tried to bring to mind the most tedious things that I could imagine. Yet my consciousness of the problem only seemed to accentuate it. I still hadn't deflated when we arrived at our destination. To preserve some modesty, I positioned the bat in front of me as we left the carriage.

On the platform at Hampton station my father met a man that he knew, a superior at his office, and he told the man that we had been to the city to select my first bat.

(In this most recent dream, the man looked less like the man that I remember from the event, or the original dream, than like Mr Sanders, who would have been my mathematics master at the time.) When this man asked if he could inspect my bat, I made such a clumsy botch of passing it to him that I drew attention to my aroused condition. All three of us were embarrassed, and the bat was passed back to me without comment. Later, as we turned into a quiet street, my father pinched me hard on the flesh at the back of my arm, telling me, You're not to be trusted. I can't take you anywhere.

When I awoke from this dream, the train was thundering across a moonsilver plain, and the pretty deaf girl was asleep with her head resting on my shoulder, so that the perfume of her silky hair invaded my nostrils, and I was bone hard for the first time in many months.

I saw that the young man opposite was wide awake, staring into the luminous countryside. At intervals he took a swig from his nearly drained bottle of vodka. When he noticed that I had woken, he offered the bottle to me with a nod and a conspiratorial smile, as if to observe that both he and I were lucky men with women. He must have seen then that I was offended by the inference that I was a man who might take advantage of an innocent situation, and tried to erase this hint of carnality by observing, She's very sweet. He spoke clearly, aware that sound would not disturb our sleeping companion.

It's a real sad thing, isn't it? Such a pretty girl. Do you have children? I'm guessing from your ring that you're a married man.

When forced to consider the matter, I see my married life unveil like the suburbs of a city seen from a train travelling in reverse; a collection of pain-tainted vignettes that become less repugnant as they shift into the middle distance. I could extend the metaphor to incorporate the stations of my wife's infidelity, but when questioned about my marriage, I generally choose to be vague and evasive, to assert that I am a traveller committed to the perspectives afforded by travel. I can believe that it's possible to remember everything, imagine anything, while I am aboard a train in motion.

I knew intuitively that none of this would interest my companion. He wanted to tell me that his father was dead, and that he would inherit his father's wine-importing business. The inheritance would make him one of the wealthiest men in the country. He wanted to tell me that it hadn't been his grandfather who disapproved of his love for a cousin, but his father who prohibited his love for an older sister. As he told me this, he examined my face, expecting it to register shock or outrage, but I was not shocked, because I have travelled, and I have known alcohol to facilitate confidences of this kind.

Now scarcely able to string a sentence together, the man declared that he had known his sister intimately since he was eleven and she thirteen, and that his business at our destination was to arrange a change of identity so that he and his sister might marry and start a new life in the west.

If I cared more, I might have told the young drunk that nothing can distance a person from integral truths. Having decided that a truth is crucial, you give it licence to hunt you down. You will be hunted down by dead fathers, betrayed mothers, by the thought of your wife naked beneath the motion of another man's buttocks.

I know that we're going to be very happy, he insisted. So happy, she and I, when we're husband and wife. Happy together.

Though he meant for me to endorse this comment, I

refrained. I know more about the thoughts prompted by a vehicle in motion than I could claim to know about happiness. Happiness is no more explicable than the rousing fragrance of the pretty deaf girl, who chose that moment to shift her head on my shoulder.

Do you suppose that she had an accident? the young man asked.

It's probably genetic, I said.

As the sun rises, the train will begin its descent from the mountains towards the distant corkscrew spires of the great city. There is nothing particularly dramatic about this elevation. Nevertheless, many first-time travellers are excited by the quality of the morning light. They reach for their cameras when they see the green-gold of rolling hills all spotted with cows and sheep. I might have done likewise once, but a real traveller knows that to capture a brief visual impression insults memory as much as it insults travel. There will always be a Y-junction on the outer perimeter of the city, and a pause before the train shifts into reverse. However you choose to situate yourself in relation to the vehicle's motion, you travel steadily and inexorably toward that place from which you hoped to have found refuge.

The associate

Richard's mother was a decent, conservative woman, and her reactions to indecency or obscenity were entirely predictable.

He would recognize the danger signs. A slammed door. His mother calling his name as she stormed through the house, searching. He might need to hide, or pretend to be ill, but sooner or later his mother would confront him with the Polaroid photograph.

Would you like to tell me where this comes from?

Where what comes from? he'd ask, feigning ignorance.

This! Where this comes from, this filth that was in an envelope in the letterbox.

His mother would shake the obscene photograph in his face. He wouldn't be able to look at it. He wouldn't be able to look his mother in the eye. But he would feel the red glow of her.

Because if you can't tell me, Richard, if you don't know what this is about, I'll have to take it to the police. Maybe the police can tell me what it's about.

It took only a small fraction of time for the scene to play itself out in Richard's mind, but he foresaw it all in minute detail.

◆

If you had been a passenger on a Sandringham train one Saturday afternoon in June, 1973, you might have seen two boys wrestling on the grass just outside Hampton station. Richard, the fat, mop-headed boy was on top, while Marco, taller and more athletic, struggled beneath him. Though Richard lacked muscle, he used his weight to keep Marco's shoulders pinned. But, having neutralized Marco's punching ability, Richard didn't know what to do with him, and the four other boys circling the fighters were becoming frustrated by the lack of violence.

Stop poofterizing an' start punching, Al yelled.

What are yers, bum chums? Mick goaded.

Then Davo shook a can of soft drink and pulled the ring-tab, hosing the fighters with Coke, and forcing them to separate.

All a piss-weak fight like that deserves, Davo announced.

Considering the fight over, Richard pulled off his jumper so that he could wring out the Coke. He was very sensitive about the skinny-rib jumper with the orange, gold and black hoops. His mother had given it to him on his thirteenth birthday the week before. Richard was wringing out the sleeve of his jumper when he was clouted across the face by a round-arm blow from behind.

Blood squirted from his nostrils in a long trail down the front of his white T-shirt. When he clasped at his nose, the blood dripped between his fingers. Richard turned to see Marco, wild-eyed, breathing deeply, showing Richard his clenched fist as he took slow backward steps.

Just don't pull that shit again, Fatguts.

Marco enjoyed nothing more than a punch-up. A month or two after this fight, he would get a skinhead haircut, and within two years he would be sent to a juvenile detention centre with a conviction for Grievous Bodily

Harm. By nineteen, he would be dead from a drug over-dose.

When Marco was back with the rest of his gang, Paul sidled up beside Richard and put a hand on his back.

OK, mate?

Just grab me jumper will ya, Richard said, trying to sound tougher than he felt.

Marco called out to Davo, who had been delegated to mind Marco's schoolbag.

You're gone if you sprayed Coke on my camera, shithead!

Richard and Paul had intended to go to the football at Moorabbin, but Paul spent his money on cigarettes. Though Richard wanted to see the game, he didn't want to go by himself, and he didn't have enough money to pay for them both. They were messing around on the tracks near Hampton station when they ran into Marco and his mates.

Usually, Richard kept out of Marco's way, but Paul moved on the fringe of Marco's gang. Paul could be a moper. A frustrated history teacher used to call him Gumby, after the plasticine character on television. He'd scream at Paul, Tell me what you think . . . what *you* think, boy! But any appeal to Paul's individuality was a waste of breath. Paul needed to be liked, but, at very least, not disliked, and he wasn't going to discriminate against anyone who might be a mate. He had a foggy vision of a future where everyone would want to be his mate, though he hadn't the slightest idea how this would be achieved. He used to say that he was going to form a band, but he never learnt to play an instrument. The only thing that he and Richard had in common was that they supported the same football team. Even then, Paul's enthusiasm for football depended on who else would be going to the game.

Paul dithered when Marco asked him to help steal some bikes from the front of Moorabbin Bowl.

You'd be in real deep shit if you got caught, mate, Richard told Paul. And it's forty minutes walk just to get there.

An' who asked you, Fatguts? Marco said, inhaling with a crude nasal snort before spitting a thick wad of mucus into Richard's face.

After the fight, Marco left with his gang, and Paul was remorseful. Don't worry about Marco, mate. He's just a fuckwit. You had him packin' till Davo got yers with the Coke.

Richard's nose had swollen. Though the bleeding had stopped, his handkerchief was saturated with blood.

Christ, I had to get Coke all over me new jumper. Mum'll kill me.

Just tell her that some dickhead did it at the football.

We should've bought a Footy Record, Richard said. Dad never believes that I went to a game unless I show him the Record with all the goals pencilled in.

They sat near the bus shelter, watching a red rattler slow on its way into Hampton station. They heard three loud bangs as the train passed over track detonators on its way to Sandringham. Paul lit a cigarette and retold the story of the fight, exaggerating the brutality and Richard's daring. He wanted to please Richard with his chronicle of the event.

I'd love to see the pigs nab those cunts with stolen bikes, Richard said.

Another half hour passed, sitting, not saying very much.

They could hear the car horns blurt when a goal was kicked in the Thirds match at Sandringham. They'd just agreed to go for a walk along Hampton beach when they saw Marco's gang returning, accompanied by Linda Balcam, a girl who was in 2C at Hampton High with Richard and Paul.

Richard knew that Paul fancied Linda. Paul was always on about how big Linda's tits were.

If her jugs are that big now, Paul used to say, they'll be fuckin' enormous when she's fifteen.

But Richard didn't care for Linda. She hung around with Marco and Al for a start, and he thought that she was dumb. Richard noticed how the teachers, especially the women teachers, would speak to Linda as if they thought she was a slut. She wasn't a slut, but she was vacant. One of the kids just filling in time between puberty and marriage.

How come you faggots are still here? Marco asked.

Where are your bikes? Paul asked, hoping to stir them.

Had better stuff to do, Davo said.

Dunno what to do with the parts we've already got, Mick said. So we all dropped in on Linda. Linda loves to get her hands on hot parts.

Double entendre was wasted on Linda. She seemed to have little idea what she was doing there, and had the look of someone being swept along by the wind skating off the bay. Richard saw her half smile in Paul's direction. Then she noticed Richard's nose.

God, what happened to you?

The fatarse was being a smartarse, Marco said.

Linda moved closer to inspect Richard's bloated nose.

Is it broken?

Don't think so, he told her.

Irritated by Linda's concern for Richard's nose, Marco told Al to throw him his schoolbag.

Reckon we should take a few happy snaps of Linda.

Orr don't! Linda objected, ruffling her sandy red hair into shape with one hand. I look somethin' shockin' without make-up.

Marco pulled a Polaroid camera out of his schoolbag, and Davo quickly moved up behind Linda, grabbing her tightly so that one hand cupped her breast, while she squirmed and told him to piss off. Then Mick moved in to unbutton Linda's jeans, while Al stood to one side shouting excitedly, Dack her! Dack her!

Shit, he's dackin' her! Paul shouted at Richard, who could see what was happening.

Fuck off! Linda spluttered.

Mick pulled her jeans down around her ankles, and then he pulled down her lemon-coloured panties. Marco moved in front of her with the camera.

Hold her legs apart, so that I can get her twat, Marco ordered.

Marco don't! Linda screamed.

Marco's finger pushed the button on the camera, and the others released their hold on Linda, who grabbed for her pants, and bellowed through her tears, Yers are all fuckin' arseholes!

Paul was still charged enough to grab Richard by the arm.

Did ya see that? Orr mate, did ya see that? What a great fanny!

Linda, with her jeans on, threw herself back on the grass, sobbing, while the gang clustered together and waited for the photo to develop. Marco peeled away the negative.

Orr, check out the snatch! Davo enthused.

Marco pronounced that the photo was a ripper. He called out to Linda.

A photo like this is worth big bucks. I could sell it for heaps at school.

Linda covered her face with her hands. Just rip it up. Yer a filthy prick, Marco.

Reckon ya mum'll be thrilled when we show her this. Hey, Mrs Balcam, your Linda's been flashin' her gash again!

Paul must have reckoned that it was time to ingratiate himself with Linda. C'mon mate, he told Marco, enough's enough. You've got your photo. You've had some fun.

Linda's having fun, Marco said. Aren't you, Linda? And you've got a real hairy snatch, haven't you, Linda?

Richard and Paul tried to approach Linda, who refused to look at any of the boys, but Marco and the others obstructed their path.

Don't worry, Linda, Marco said. We won't show your mother. You can have your photo back just as soon as we've all had a handful.

Richard might have thought that Linda was dumb, but she had anticipated Marco's demand, and had made her choice even before the options were presented to her. Still crying, she moved like someone resigned to get the worst over with quickly. Linda followed Marco, Mick, Davo, and Al behind the bus shelter.

Sometimes Richard could pretend to know something about sex— he knew all the words and what they meant— but in truth he knew very little. He was like most of the kids his age, surviving on bluff, and third-hand information.

Do ya reckon they'll gang bang her?

Nah, just give her a finger, I reckon, Paul said disdainfully.

Maybe we better go, Richard said, but not with any conviction.

Paul wasn't moving. Let's just see what happens, mate.

They heard the boys laughing from behind the bus

shelter. They heard Linda squeal, Go easy! Twenty minutes or more passed before the group emerged. Marco had
his arm around Linda's shoulders. Her cheeks were red and
wet.

Fuckin' goer. Yer shoulda got a sniff, Davo told Paul.

Didn't feel like it, Paul said.

Reckon you two poofters have never seen a fanny, Marco
said. Get a whiff of these, he said, pushing two fingers into
Richard's face.

Richard tried to look impassive. He wanted to sound
streetwise and emphatic like a television cop, like Gerard
Kennedy on *Division 4*.

You're an arsehole, Marco.

Marco paused as he stood opposite Richard. Then he
smacked him across the nose with an open hand, so that
Richard's nostrils again squirted blood.

Hope you've taken good care of me camera, Marco said,
picking up his bag and shoving it into Richard's hands. I'd
take real good care of that if I was you.

Should kick fuckin' shit out of your camera, Richard
mumbled, his eyes turned to the ground.

What was that, fatarse? Marco said, mockingly cupping
a hand over his ear. Do what you like. But you explain to
your mum why she's getting pictures of muffburger
dropped into her letterbox.

As Marco moved away with his cronies, Richard pictured
his mother opening an envelope with the Polaroid photograph of Linda inside. It only took a fraction of time for
the whole scene to appear to him in horrifying detail. The
slamming doors. The photograph waved in his face. The
inquisition. He tried not to betray his anxiety. He tried to
concentrate on the cold bite of the wind against his throb-
bing nose. The blood dripped from his chin onto Marco's

schoolbag. More than anything, Richard wanted to be home in bed, with the blankets pulled up over his head.

Better just to keep your mouth shut, mate, Paul said. Marco's all talk. He won't do anything.

Richard swung Marco's bag in a big arc as if intending to fling it onto the railway line.

Forget about it, mate, Paul said. It's nothin'. She's just a slut anyway.

But Richard wasn't thinking about Linda. He couldn't have cared less about her at that point. He wasn't worried where his blood dripped. He was thinking about his mother opening an envelope addressed to her. He was picturing his mother confronting him with a Polaroid close-up of a girl's genitals, asking him if he knew where it came from. He was recoiling from her awful disappointment.

Are you two poofters bringin' me fuckin' bag, or what?

Richard put Marco's schoolbag under his arm, and he and Paul followed Marco's gang down the path that ran alongside the railway line. Richard wished that he had a lumber jacket like Paul's, with a fleecy collar that he could raise to keep out the icy wind gusting off the bay.

*O*ur *swimmer*

Seeing films has corrupted the way that we remember things. Our minds will now perform sophisticated technical operations. We can isolate the subject in the frame, we can enhance or colorize, we can edit our memories into dazzling montage sequences. Now I find that when I remember Marianne Topp, I see her moving in a stylized, filmic way, as if some mental process has extracted every second frame of memory to create a more artistic, expressionistic version of my emotional attachment to her.

Marianne was an extraordinary looking girl, her dark hair so often pulled up in a bun that emphasized the curve of her neck, her cheeks, and her red-charged lips. Yet the essence of my attraction to her wasn't the way that she looked or moved. It was Marianne's voice that stole my heart— a low, carnal mutter, not so studied as the Mae West mutter, but with the same coarse-textured depth. Her voice had a natural insinuation that sent blood racing to vital outposts. And she fully understood the power of this weapon. Her speech was always so measured and deliberate. Everything about Marianne was perfectly composed.

I was browsing in Chapters Bookshop, scanning the blurb of a paperback. The book must have been *Oranges*

Are Not The Only Fruit, and she must have been looking over my shoulder.

If you like Jeanette Winterson, you should read *The Passion*.

I turned to face the voice, to tell the woman with the pulverizing voice that I'd read *The Passion* and adored it. Then I saw that the speaker was Marianne Topp, whom I'd only ever worshipped from a distance, and her mouth had broken into a soft, slightly embarrassed smile, and I was in love then, instantly. I was seventeen, and, like just about everyone else, I was in love with Marianne Topp.

Marianne Topp kept so much to herself that people seldom associated her with her mother Beatrice, the most forceful presence in Hampton. When Mrs Topp's newspaper was left to soak in the rain, she made sure that the paperboy responsible was punished. Wayne Burgess was locked up in stocks for two days. This punishment would have gone on for a week, but the matriarch relented when the boy's doctor testified to his epilepsy.

I was playing cricket with Sam Morrissey the day that Sam was found out. Beatrice Topp discovered that Sam was the author of obscene letters sent to her daughter at the Topps' Favril Street home. Two senior teachers ripped Sam off the field and took him to be interrogated by Mrs Topp. You didn't need to be Einstein to predict the outcome. My mother went to console Sam's mum, who was a friend she knew from tuckshop duty.

Having confessed to the crime, Sam was condemned to death. On the day of the execution, the Principal pulled six boys out of the matriculation geography class. He took them to the school oval, where they were told to construct a pyre out of old desks and broken chairs. Mrs Topp decreed that Sam should be taken up in a cherry-picker, from which he would be lowered by rope onto the flaming pyre below.

All of Hampton gathered for the execution, which had been scheduled for just after sunset on March twenty-ninth. Mr Paterson, the sportsmaster, was assigned the task of restraining Sam in the basket of the cherry-picker. He was an unpleasant man well suited to the unpleasant task. Sam's bellows were so loud that Mr Paterson was forced to gag him while Mrs Topp read a list of his offences to the crowd. She was wearing her favourite purple jumpsuit.

Mrs Topp said that Sam had written anonymous letters in which her daughter— she didn't name which daughter, but everyone knew she meant the eldest, Marianne— was described as a cheap slag who'd jazzed so many old men that her mother had been forced to install a condom machine at the foot of her bed. Few of us had ever heard such a vile attack against an innocent girl. When Beatrice Topp called for a volunteer to light the pyre, dozens of outraged Hamptonians rushed forward.

Flames speared out into the night sky. Sparks and embers wafted off above the orange-faced gathering. Dramatic relief gave the yellow cherry-picker the appearance of a sad mechanical giraffe. When Mrs Topp nodded, Mr Paterson eased Sam out the side of the bucket. For a few seconds, it seemed as though Sam was trying to swim across the sky. He flailed and shrieked as he dangled on the rope being lowered toward the rising flames.

Finally, Mrs Topp raised an arm to halt the execution. Sam was reprieved. His death sentence was commuted to permanent banishment from Hampton, and after that evening he was never seen in the suburb again. Not so long ago, someone told me that he's gone on to do valuable research work in immunology. But we'd all got the message.

If you took Beatrice Topp lightly, you'd live to regret it. It might be pointless for me to tell you all of this. You really can't conceive of such power unless you've experienced it first hand.

Ruthless as she was, Mrs Topp was not a political leader. No one elected her, and official authority resided with the mayor. But Mrs Topp held sway in Hampton. She represented our suburb at the summits that detailed the latest advances.

I remember how impatient we were for her return from the International Geometrical Forum in New York. We expected that Mrs Topp would come back with the New Knowledge. Everything we thought certain could be stood on its head by some astonishing development; the square triangle, or the refutation of Pythagoras.

That was the winter of unprecedented snows. The winds blasted up from the Antarctic and snap-froze birds in flight. Port Phillip Bay iced over for the first time in memory. Children skated across the rough surface, and fishermen dropped lines through holes in the thick ice. You'd see vandals strip palings off fences to fuel the bonfires they lit on the beach. Smelly Old Ryan, who lived in the telephone box outside the post office, was taken in by church people who feared that he would freeze to death, but they were so chilled by his incessant prophesying that they passed him on to the Community Welfare Officer.

Old Ryan bellowed that we were going to be buried alive, that God was revisiting us with the fruits of our mediocrity. He didn't actually use the word Repent!, but you knew what he was getting at. Not that we would have repented. We were too curious, too used to these astonishments to be fazed by them. So we waited for Beatrice Topp and did what we could to keep warm.

I often played squash with my friend Yuri at the fitness centre by Hampton railway station. After a match, we swam a few lengths, or sat by the pool and watched Marianne Topp cruise through her 10 000 metre training regime. We were entranced by the rhythmic thrust of her muscular arms breaking the surface. We fixed our gaze on the dark tufts of hair under her arms, and the glorious dark locks she dragged through the blue water, and the sheer magnificence of the so-womanly body packed into Marianne's black one-piece swimsuit.

Like most of the students and staff at Hampton High, I worshipped the enigmatic Marianne Topp. What's more, we were expected to worship her.

At school assembly, the Principal would detail Marianne's latest achievements in the pool. He told us that Marianne had swum nine seconds inside Janet Evans' official World Record for 800 metres freestyle. Even her final 400 metres was two seconds faster than Janet Evans' record for that distance.

Marianne Topp, the Principal told us, is a uniquely talented young woman who upholds the finest traditions of the school. If you look closely at her performances, you will see that Marianne is a negative splitter. She's even stronger at the end of a race than she is at the beginning. In that, he emphasized, there is a lesson for us all.

After a spirited round of cheering, I heard a boy behind me say that he'd give anything to be Marianne Topp's bicycle seat, and when I turned around to see who it was, I saw that Mr Simonescu, the woodwork teacher, had heard the remark, and was smiling lasciviously.

All the teachers were hot for Marianne, the women as much as the men, but Marianne made a point of ignoring their attentions. She did them a favour. Being a teacher wouldn't have saved them from the cherry-picker.

We all knew that Marianne Topp would have been an Olympic gold medallist if her mother had allowed her to represent Australia, but Mrs Topp was a fierce anti-nationalist. She would have had Hampton secede from the Australian Commonwealth if it was possible for a suburb to secede.

Australia is lazy and complacent, Mrs Topp would say, too satisfied with living vicariously through its sporting heroes. Hampton has to make itself a model for what's possible.

For Marianne to have represented Australia would have been an unthinkable treachery.

Nevertheless, the school celebrated its negative splitter in a very Australian fashion. The administration building was two storeys high, with a vast expanse of white wall facing to the west. The Principal instructed the senior art teacher to design a mural portrait of Marianne Topp. Each day, a group of fourth formers was sent out to bring the project to life. It took them a full term to complete an immensely beautiful, six-metre square portrait of our swimmer. Each of her lips was the size of a tall sixth form boy lying on his side, and every lunchtime you would see a cluster of students gathered below Marianne's image. Swooning.

Marianne had one or two friends, but she wasn't part of a group. She didn't identify with heroes or pursuits the way that some kids identified with Nick Cave, or football, or weekend alcoholism. She gave the impression that she was entirely self-sufficient, that she had everything she needed emotionally, or thought that she had. I don't mean to suggest that Marianne was stuck-up or arrogant. She was guarded. Her smile, magnificent as it was, was a this-far-and-no-further smile.

What happened to Mr Topp? I asked my mother.

She dispensed with him.

Then how could she get to have so much power without any backing? What made her want to take over?

I don't think that she ever planned to take over. She just seemed capable at a time when people needed someone who seemed capable. She was co-opted by our neediness. We snaffled her.

But what could we need so much that we were prepared to be treated like shit?

I didn't say need. I said neediness. It's a different thing altogether.

The ice began to crack and melt. The skies turned a darker, cloudless blue. A rumour plague broke out. There were rumours that the Geometrical Summit had collapsed. The participants were said to have been devastated by the discovery of a previously unknown real number between sixteen and seventeen. The seventeen year olds among us feared that the new number might affect eligibility to take the driving test at eighteen.

Marianne was due to turn eighteen in October. When she broke her own unofficial world record for the 400 Freestyle in September, the Principal called a half-holiday. Students wishing to commemorate Marianne's achievement were encouraged to visit Ron Dorfmann, the tattooist in Hampton Village.

I remember a very proud Jane Nelson unbuttoning her blouse to show us where Ron had etched the letters **M.T.**

above the nipple on her perfectly shaped left breast. Poor Jane was mortified when we explained the double entendre.

But Marianne-madness was like that. Someone discovered that she loved expensive Belgian chocolate, and within days Hampton post office was jammed with parcels of chocolate addressed to Ms M. Topp. At times, Marianne seemed to be the only person in Hampton not affected by Marianne-madness. We were all hopelessly distracted, waiting for her mother to return, and waiting for Marianne to betray just a hint of vulnerability, a vacuum of neediness that we could be sucked into.

I told Yuri that he was crazy to spend his savings buying chocolate for Marianne. I told him that he was inviting her contempt. But I never confessed to Yuri that I slipped $200 to a waitress at Coriander's Deli for a white coffee cup that still had Marianne's lipstick print on its rim. A perfect smear of Black Tulip.

Looking back at my chance meeting with Marianne in Chapters Bookshop, I see things that self-consciousness prevented me from seeing at the time. In flickery, stylized motion I see the fraction of a second when Marianne forgot about the impression she was making, and became someone capable of speaking her adoration for literature. She put her emotions on the line.

I hold that moment in freeze-frame. We are connected, perhaps ridiculously, by the strength of our mutual feeling for the work of an author neither of us will meet. We are as powerless before this feeling as any character in a fiction by Jeanette Winterson. How is it that I can now isolate this feeling and find the audacity to call it love?

A few days later, I was standing in the shaded quadrangle between school buildings, hanging out with Yuri and some other friends, when Marianne Topp strode between clusters of gawping students to present me with a novel, *Love in the Time of Cholera* by Gabriel Garcia Marquez. No particular sign of affection, or even eye contact, just, You might like to read this, before she disappeared through the crowd.

Thanks . . . Marianne, I called out after her, scarcely able to believe that I'd spoken her name out loud. My friends had lost the power of speech entirely.

Inside the front cover of the hardback novel was a note written on a slip of paper. Marianne's handwriting was as stylish as she was, and equally impenetrable. I spent the best part of that afternoon deciphering her short message. '*After Hours* is playing at the Colosseum on Saturday night. You can meet me in the foyer. M'

The Colosseum was a very grand name for a fleapit cinema that used to stand opposite the post office, where Safeway supermarket is now. The pavement outside the cinema was a favourite hang-out for warring philosophers. If you were short of entertainment on a Saturday night, you could practically guarantee a violent stoush between the followers of Quine and the Wittgenstein loyalists.

One old woman always used to sit next to the doorway of the cinema holding a placard, DEFEND COPERNICUS! When someone asked her to do this, she let out a machine-gun blurt, The New Knowledge is a farce! The New Knowledge is a lie! Topp must be stopped! The New Knowledge is a farce!

My nerves were shocking. I was back and forth to the toilet. What on earth was I doing having a date with Marianne Topp? My stomach was buckling. I tried to calm myself by singing. I love singing, but the only songs that came to mind were songs about panic, and apprehension, and death. Who the fuck did I think I was to be meeting Marianne Topp at the cinema? I brushed my teeth at least a dozen times, and brushed my tongue as often.

Outside class, Marianne nearly always wore black, sometimes black and white, very occasionally a bright red jacket, but mostly shades of black to match her hair. Which is not to forget the deep, lascivious red of her lips.

Hi, Richard. Have you been waiting long?

I didn't want to admit that I'd been in the foyer since the manager unbolted the front doors. I might have grown a beard while I'd been waiting there.

I don't remember anything about *After Hours*. We hardly spoke before the film. Marianne saw a woman she knew and spoke to her for ten minutes, while I smiled an idiot smile, and shifted my weight from foot to foot. I've never been a student of body language, but I knew enough to realize that this engagement wasn't about tit-feeling in the dark, or even hand-holding, which was just as well because someone had installed a sprinkler system in my palms.

What I do remember is that Marianne wore a fantastic, subtle perfume that activated with the rise of her body temperature. Two-thirds of the way through the feature, my nose got hooked on an updraught of irresistible scent, and I was so far lost in Swoonsville that Marianne had to send out a search party when the film ended.

She must have known what she was doing to me, but what did she want? Not a kiss, though I would have sold my parents into slavery to kiss Marianne's full red lips. I thought then that my neediness, my undisguised adoration, might have been a quaint joke to her, that she was drawing strength or resolve from my own obvious weakness. But now I am inclined to believe that she wanted someone to trust, but didn't dare cross the line to a territory where her fears and desires would be exposed.

I walked her home. We said very little. A few comments about the books we'd read, and the films we'd seen.

I see you at the pool, she said.

Well, yes. Actually, I'm a drowner.

There was the slightest hint of a smile. I know, she said. You ought to get some coaching.

When I asked her if she knew when her mother would come home, she became uncomfortable and didn't answer. I certainly wasn't going to interrogate her, to ask her what it was like to be Beatrice Topp's daughter, or to be so often home alone with her two sisters. Instead, I asked her what she'd do when she left school.

I just have to get out of Hampton. I'm suffocating here.

C'mon, I joked, where in the world would you find somewhere more exciting than Hampton? I never cease to be amazed by this place.

It's possible to have too much imagination, she said.

We were at the front gate of her house then. Her German shepherd was barking. Marianne moved her hand so that it briefly touched the back of mine.

Thanks, that was nice, she said.

I reconstruct this scene in my mind. I doubt that I could have played it any differently, not even if I'd known that it was the last time that I'd ever see Marianne.

Shortly before dawn, two days later, a light plane flew into Hampton, using a four-lane stretch of Ludstone Street as a landing strip. When it took off thirty minutes later, the plane struggled to squeeze through a gap between overhead power lines. Among its passengers were Marianne Topp and her two younger sisters, Beth and Cicely.

The Topp girls left in a big rush. Their house was a mess. Hampton people speculated that they may have been taken against their will, but it was impossible to compare the scene they left behind with how they lived ordinarily because the Topps had never invited anyone into their home.

Their moonlight departure became widely known when Federal Police disclosed that they had been keeping watch on the activities of Beatrice Topp. Federal agents alleged that she had been in Hong Kong conducting unauthorized land deals. At a time when she ought to have been gleaning the New Knowledge from the International Geometrical Summit, Beatrice Topp had been flogging sections of Hampton to a consortium of Asian and American business interests. No one knew what had been sold, or the legal status of her transactions, but one thing was certain, Hamptonians could no longer imagine that they lived at the centre of their own small world.

A friend with access to police intelligence suggested that Mrs Topp had fled to Switzerland or Kenya, and that she had arranged for her daughters to be brought to her. That was as close as the police ever got to locating any of the family.

In her absence, Hampton's matriarch was tried by criminal courts, being prosecuted first for fraud, then for various misappropriations. As the hostility toward her grew, new charges were brought. Soon, Beatrice Topp was being tried for crimes that hadn't seemed so much like crimes at the time; abuse of public trust, conspiracy, and false imprisonment. Each week, another case against Mrs Topp passed through the court, and she was sentenced to a further term of imprisonment. And so it went on, till whatever Hampton needed to purge itself of had been thoroughly evacuated.

If anything, the airbrushing of Marianne Topp was

crueller than the vilification of her mother. It was permissible to speak your outrage at the treachery of Mrs Topp, but Marianne's name could not be spoken. It was as if she had been a heroine of the Third Reich, or a collaborationist entertainer in Vichy France. Marianne's name was removed from the school's honour boards, her photographs taken down from the corridor walls, and the same students who had produced the superb mural portrait of Marianne were sent up the scaffolds to slather it over with garish yellow paint.

It is a difficult period for me to speak about. Shock and confusion kept me at one step removed from feelings that might have been totally destructive. I seem to have lived in a permanent dream, a festival of imagined departures and passionate reunions.

My most frequent dream was one in which Marianne taps on my window late at night, and tells me that she has to go. I am so overwhelmed by this that I can't question why, or express my feelings for her, or say any of the proper things. There is no kiss. But in the dream it seems enough that she's chosen to tell me.

She is rushing for the plane when I remember that I still have her book. What about your Marquez? I call. She halts, and turns, and there is the miraculous coalition of the two gestures that I least expect from Marianne Topp; a relaxed, totally unrestrained smile, and a single tear. A moment in which everything is exposed entirely. I want you to have it, she tells me, before rushing to her appointment at the makeshift airstrip.

I *did* have Marianne's book, and I've read it many times in the intervening years. *Love in the Time of Cholera* turned out to be a novel about the postponement of fated love.

The two lovers finally unite, gloriously and miraculously, when it least seems possible. How many times have I read Marianne and I into that scenario? I want more than anything to believe that she chose to leave behind the Marquez novel because it articulated her most fervent hopes for our relationship. In spite of everything, we would one day be reunited.

But I'm not such a fool that I can't admit the possibility of coincidence. Who can say that Marianne gave even a moment's thought to how I might construe or misconstrue a subtext? Maybe it was just an accident that I had her book when she was forced to leave.

Six years have passed. I often wonder whether Marianne kept swimming. I keep a close eye on major swimming championships. Only in the last eighteen months have swimmers begun to approach the unofficial world records that Marianne swam when she was Hampton's darling.

After a long period of procrastination, the Federal Government decided to compensate the business people who had been stung by Beatrice Topp's illegal transactions. Though this spared Hampton from foreign ownership, the suburb couldn't insulate itself against changes brought by market forces. The cinema was forced to close, and the High School that was so much the heart of our community was sold to developers. The High School buildings were demolished, to be replaced by gauche but costly new residences.

During the demolition of the two-storey administration building, I became friendly with Josef, a plump, black-bearded Romanian who operated a massive bulldozer. I managed to persuade Josef to gently tilt a portion of the west wall so that it could be recovered with its yellow-coated brickwork intact. The retrieved expanse of wall, one and a half metres high and three metres wide, stands on my back patio, leaning against the garage.

After receiving advice from conservators at the State Museum, I began to excavate a portion of the Marianne Topp mural. It's a laborious process, scouring away the thick coat of yellow plastic paint, while trying to keep the submerged level of portrait undamaged. Friends joke about my enterprise, and refer to the wall as The Hampton Shroud.

Gradually, the outline of Marianne's fabulous red lips has begun to emerge. When they are finally retrieved, I might use the lips in photo-composites or treatments, but just now it is enough that they will be retrieved. There is a romantic side of me that wants to believe that everything worth retrieving can be retrieved.

Still, I have a cynical side too. My cynicism reminds me that it's not a Michaelangelo that I toil on, but the rushed work of spotty fourth form art students. In many ways, my quest is as pathetic as it is heroic.

The air got terribly cold when I was working on Marianne's upper lip last Sunday. I could barely flex my fingers to operate the spatula. Feeling something brush against my ear, I looked up from my work to see a brief, majestic flurry of snowflakes. My heart almost seized with joy. This was the first snow that I'd seen in Hampton since that extraordinary winter when the Bay iced over and small birds snap-froze in flight.

Extracts from
The Creative Process

DISCRETION

Because he is a character who does as his author wishes, Richard creeps downstairs to investigate the noise, even though it is late and the house has been blacked out by the electrical storm raging overhead.

Richard is inordinately conscious of the sound of his own breathing. He hears each creaky shift of the boards beneath his feet. When lightning illuminates the downstairs lounge, he imagines that he glimpses an assailant waiting for him in the darkness.

The candles are not where he remembers having put them. I'm sure I put them in the kitchen cupboard, Richard tells himself. No, it must have been the cupboard in the hall.

Richard is holding his breath, and feeling his way down the corridor, when he hears a noise from Marianne's bedroom. Marianne had told him that she would be going to Point Lonsdale for the weekend. Richard tries to ease open her door, silently, but the old brass knob rotates in his hand, and when he exerts greater force, the door jolts open and slams against a bookcase.

Forgetting the blackout, Richard reaches for the light switch, but as he does so he is arrested by a strangely familiar odour.

Jesus Christ, what is that smell?

The precise nature of that smell comes to him in an instant, mysteriously, a harpoon fired from a past world into this. Richard identifies it as the smell of Tom Piper Canned Ham, something that he hasn't smelt since he was a boy at Hampton State School.

In this fraction of time, Richard recalls the strange key device which opened the can, and how the jellied slab of ham made a slurpy-fart noise when his mother excised it with a fork. He would then watch her cut it in thick rectangular chunks to be placed into fresh white-bread sandwiches.

How can I have gone all these years without remembering the smell of Tom Piper Canned Ham? Richard asks himself.

Richard is in Marianne's room, in the darkness, the storm overhead, remembering a time when he was sent home from school to fetch sandwiches his sister had forgotten to pack in her lunchbox, the sharpness of the sun then, and the aftertaste of too-quickly-swigged school milk . . . He is remembering all of this when a man emerges from behind a wardrobe and clubs Richard over the back of the head with an axe, killing him instantly.

When this story appears, there will be no mention of Richard's recollection of Tom Piper Canned Ham. We will experience Richard as a colourless victim, the sum of his undistracted nervousness. His memory of canned ham would intrude on a story that belongs to the killer, Jack. We understand this process of excision as the author's discretion.

Perhaps the author knows that the killer has recognized this smell also, only he identifies it as the smell of fresh-cut lawns on humid Sunday afternoons in Sydney. Covered in blood and chunks of brain, Jack would wish to remember the childhood errands, half-skipped, half-run, to the local milkbar in Eastwood. He refrains. As much as he would like to forget the body and remember the lawns, the murderer knows too well the fate of characters who stray from the worn path of fictional reality.

SUBSTANCE

In this game, everything is about balance, or the lack of it. The skills we have are largely intuitive. Experience comes into it, but it's not as if experience will give you a set of rules to operate by. Experience will tell you that you are upsetting the balance of a composition, though you won't know what form that composition is meant to take, or your exact relationship to the central elements of the composition. Sometimes, you might be crucial to a deliberate imbalance, or to the demonstration of an absurd illogicality. And your job is always to make it look natural, as though it couldn't have turned out any other way. It really shits me that our skills are so under-appreciated—here in Australia, particularly. You're treated like a functionary, or a labourer. Or worse: an actor.

This is going to sound conceited, but neither of us is happy with what we are doing here, waiting in the wings for a bit part in someone else's story. We consider ourselves to be fully-rounded heroic types. Only a few years back, Marianne was the first-person narrator in a novel short-listed for the Miles Franklin. You look at some of the women who have central roles in this novel—Is it a novel,

Approximate Life? They disappear, they're abducted, they're reduced to the memory of a forgettable kiss or a lipstick smear. They're not real women. They're caricatures of real Australian women. Marianne has substance.

And your professionalism is always being held against you. We're told that there's nothing suitable, because authors have stereotyped us as self-referential, post-modern characters. You hear it everywhere, You're good. I really like what you've done, but this is 1995. We need something different. And you can't persuade them that you can only be different, show that you can be different, if you're *allowed* to be different. You've got to be given a chance.

I've proven that I can do naturalism, dirty realism, and magical realism— I've blown into a handkerchief and had my snot turn into butterflies— but now it's, We loved that Argentinian business, we loved your butterflies, but can you do magical realism with a Western Australian accent and make it sound convincing? Christ, who could do that? Not even Mr Humbert Humbert himself could do that.

We're fall guys. We're always being forced to pay for management mismanagements. If someone ever listened to our opinions, we could cut out a lot of the shit that gets onto the bookshelves. Instead, we're asked to grapple with ridiculous vogues like this latest one, 'autobiographical expressionism'. As far as I can tell, and you can quote me on this (when did you last read an Australian novel and find a character worth quoting?), this autobiographical expressionism is just a feeble excuse for the author to recycle slabs from his diary, and turn old girlfriends, and his letters to old girl-friends, into footnotes in literary history. Since when did fiction need real people dressed up as characters? I remember when fiction was about fictional characters who were *proud* to be fictional characters.

Sure, we could go overseas. I've had offers. But it's like Marianne says, we're Australian characters with an Australian perspective, that's our genius. We'll just have to guts it out, and hope that it doesn't get so that only ethnic minorities score the big roles in the major novels. Given a chance, I could have been Jack Meredith. Oscar, in *Oscar and Lucinda*, I could have done that. No shit. But what do you get offered? If you're not being a third-rate Australian impersonating a second-rate Yank, you're asked to be a sleazy Kundera-type Euro, spouting platitudes about the movement of history while you're bedding some young dish whose pubes haven't curled. I know this sounds like a king-sized whinge, but I'm worried where the future's heading. Will Marianne have to be some gumshoe lesbian detective just to get a major credit?

I've spoken to publishers, I've had my agent speak to publishers, What about a character-based novel? What about something real and feisty like *Joan Makes History*, where Joan can just up and say 'Fuck you' to the author and go wherever she wants? The publishers won't hear of it. Critical pressures. Institutional pressures. Any excuse, I've heard them all. Personally, I blame grants.

It hurts me to see Marianne waiting here in a nurse's uniform. She'll get ten and a half pages teaching a reformed junkie how to shit again. And me, two cliché-infested pages as the father of a boy who steps on a syringe. You're a professional, and you put your all into it, but it's not Poppy. It's not Alethea Hunt. It's not Jack Meredith.

THE EXERCYCLE

Midway through last year, I made a discovery. I was in the family room, riding my exercycle, when sentences began to shoot into my brain. One sentence flowed seamlessly into another, and they were brilliant sentences, the insights as dramatic as they were unexpected. However, when I leapt off the bike to write down the lines that had come to me, my inspiration dried up. I still had my narrative voice and situation, dazzling phrases that I could record, but my unimpeded stream of sentences had ceased streaming.

Not long after, I was seated on the cycle completing my twenty kilometre daily regime, when the sentences again stole into my head, prescient and majestic, taking up where they left off. They came at such a rate that I was at once trying to remember them and allow them to flow. I asked my partner Catherine to bring me a pen and paper, and, still cycling, I began to transcribe the paragraphs that were being mysteriously dictated. During this process, I noticed something striking. If my peddling slowed below a certain speed, the quality of the language would deteriorate. If I sped up, the narrative began to lose sense and logic. So long as I maintained a speed that was precise to a decimal point, I was on the road to literary fame.

Quite apart from the awkwardness of having to write while peddling, there was the difficulty of maintaining speed. I feared that I might lack the fitness to become a great writer. But I had to accept that this was my uncorked genie. Just as some writers find inspiration in opium, and others find it in the memory of a half-dunked sweet biscuit, I came to believe that the most creative portion of my brain was activated when I peddled my exercycle at a precise speed.

My sense of having achieved a breakthrough was endorsed when a publisher offered me a five-figure advance on the basis of fifty pages I sent to her after my first jaunts.

I began to speculate whether I might have stumbled upon a secret already known to the major writers. Maybe this was how Toni Morrison, Milan Kundera, and Alice Munro had composed all along. But the thing was, and I say this with due regard for modesty, the fiction I wrote while cycling at the literary limit was far more astonishing, diverting, and substantial than anything my heroes could have written. I was embarrassed by the power of my prose. My publisher must have been embarrassed also. She volunteered to raise the advance even before she received a second instalment of my novel.

Just when the future couldn't have seemed brighter, my discovery struck a hitch.

You are waiting for me to tell you that thieves stole my exercycle, or that the chain slipped, that I had a heart attack, or that the speedometer began to malfunction, but my hitch was a theoretical oversight. I'd taken note of the exact speed to optimize literary production, and I assumed that this speed connected with some mysterious function or chemical change within my brain. What I failed to imagine was that I had accidentally stumbled on something of even greater significance— a universal law of literary production. And not just literary production— *masterpiece* production.

This unfortunate extrapolation revealed itself one evening as I sat listening to the stereo; it might have been Ed Kuepper or R.E.M., I don't remember exactly. What matters is that I was pondering things unliterary as Catherine did her bit on the exercycle.

With so much money and praise coming into the household, Catherine was curious about the optimal speed, and set about maintaining that speed for a kilometre or two. She had barely cycled more than 500 metres at the required speed when she called me to bring a pad and pen.

Catherine loves to take the piss, and I enjoy giving her the opportunity, because her playful moods add a dimension to our sex life. So I stood to one side while Catherine cycled and scribbled, scribbled and cycled. I was smugly confident that she would have written 'Fuck you, Richard!' five hundred times by the end of her epic journey.

I would have been happier to have read five hundred 'Fuck yous'.

What she had written was astonishing. The force of Catherine's prose left my own nascent masterpiece in the shade. The worst thing was, Catherine has never wanted to be a famous writer. She's a forensic pathologist; a technician, and a remarkably skilled one. Catherine realized even before I did that her confirmation of the cycling speed to maximize literary consciousness had effectively undermined thousands of years of courage, toil, and literary talent. What we've just done, she told me—and you'll appreciate that only a forensic pathologist could put it quite like this—is sodomize the corpse of Charles Dickens.

I looked at my exercycle differently after that.

Educationists have it wrong when they warn the young about the danger of drugs. They depict the drug user as a dehumanized desperado, and suggest that a drug like heroin will automatically give users the appearance of a sick panda. The real problem with a drug like heroin is that it offers sensations that are too good for the world we live in. Heroin can provide a sublime sense of wellbeing that does not correspond with ordinary experience, so removing perspective from the quality of that existence. The sad truth is that our pissy lives aren't really good enough for the mind-altering substances that we use to enliven them. Efforts to incorporate the two worlds too frequently result in corporate takeover. My point is this: it's the duty of artists and writers to supply a middle ground, to chip away, to offer the odd new way of looking at things. Artists should be *of* the world, yet beyond it, occasionally tossing the pink streamer that makes our drab meaninglessness tolerable.

Once I realized that the consequence of my discovery would be the devaluation of all literature, I had no choice but to do the honourable thing. I withdrew the offer of the novel, and returned the advance to my publisher. Catherine and I destroyed the passages that we had written. We decided then to never disclose the optimal cycling speed for literary production. To disclose the speed would be the modern equivalent of putting a torch to the Library of Alexandria. By allowing any fool to be Shakespeare, you murder Shakespeare.

Let the uninspired telling of this tale stand as testimony to my lack of talent. Unfortunately, my genius is tied to the creative endorphins released when cycling at the optimal speed. If anything, my literary career has declined since I made my discovery. Now I perceive with acute clarity how banal and inadequate my unenhanced works are. I'm fortunate to have Catherine's support, and I do not seek fame in literary circles for acting selflessly. However, should you read this story and consider yourself a more talented writer than I am, you might wish to send a token of your appreciation care of the publisher. If nothing else, my sacrifice has added value to your labours. And you can expect your generosity to receive the ideal reciprocation, since you know that when I read your genuine works of art, I'll read them while cycling at a speed that optimizes appreciation of true literary achievement.

Going the growl

The Compensations of Style

The manager of the pet shop in Hampton Village told me:
Mr Thompson, you've got vehicle owners, and you've got
pet owners. A kid travelling on roller-blades is after a
guinea pig or a rabbit. Someone who drives a Honda Civic
should buy a parrot or a cocker spaniel. But a BMW man
needs a lion, and you look to me like a BMW man.

Afterwards, I knew that I'd been flattered by a
salespitch, but that hardly touched my feelings of pride as
I drove down the main street of Hampton with a lion in
the passenger seat of my Datsun.

Homesickness

My agent Judy tried to dissuade me from writing about my
'lion phase', arguing that the lion was a misjudgement that
does little credit to a person of my intelligence. When she
saw how determined I was, she insisted that I disguise my
identity by publishing the memoir under my occasional
pseudonym, Tim Richards. I don't think that I have been

able to communicate to her my view that I was writing a story about a very peculiar form of personal embarrassment, a condition that I would now refer to as Quantum Embarrassment. The term relates the difficulty I had in understanding how the fear of impotence contaminated my view of the world.

Had I been a reader confronted with a story about a young man who purchased a lion, I would have immediately begun to ask, What would a psychoanalyst like Freud or Lacan say about all of this? What does the lion represent? Yet when I came to purchase a lion myself, I was quite incapable of self-scrutiny, or recognizing the desperate frustration that seemed so obvious to my friends. I was told recently that a close friend, Catherine O'Shaunessy, had screen-printed a limited edition of **Richard Thompson's Identity Crisis** T-shirts. The shirts featured a cartoon of a very Viennese lion psychoanalyzing a puzzled young man. At the time, I wouldn't have seen the humour in this at all.

Still, there's no use denying the truth. I bought a pet lion.

It was early 1990 and my career as a writer was going nowhere. I had decided to move back to Hampton to live in the same weatherboard house where my family had lived when I was a kid. I had soft-focus memories of Hampton as a quiet suburb—more like a village really—full of birds and trees, an asylum by the sea where a man could erase a long sequence of intimate disappointments and get things rolling again.

Everything seemed to fuck-up at the same time. I'd been commissioned to adapt Julia Cortez's novel *Approximate Life* for the screen, and I couldn't get a handle on the project. The work was going so badly that the producer mentioned hiring another writer. He had already returned the first draft with the comments, 'Richard, this is fine in substance— I've got no problems with your structure— but it needs to be more audacious, more virile. This draft lacks the one thing that Julia Cortez's novel is soaked with: personal style. Be more distinctive! You need to surprise yourself!'

I'd already had all the surprises I could take. A weird misunderstanding had just ended my long friendship with Tracey. Several years before this, Tracey and I had been lovers, a dismal month of ineffectual lovemaking that our friendship had somehow managed to survive. Even when Tracey became involved with other men, she and I could still speak frankly about our desires. I can't say what prompted her sudden determination to misunderstand me. All I'd done was tell her that I wanted children. I don't see how she could have taken that as a sexual overture. All of a sudden, she refused to see me, or speak with me. I was desperately confused. I even began to worry that she'd construed my statement to mean that I was a man who *wanted* children.

I'd hoped that going home would end this procession of misery, but the shift only prompted a sequence of vivid, confronting dreams. Disturbed, aggressive dreams where I would assault strange women. Other dreams where I would disappoint my parents, who would arrive just as I was engaged in feral sex with feral women. Dreams where I would be sexually humiliated by women who seemed to be composites of women that I knew. I'd appear helpless and naked in front of them, before being torn apart by their disdain.

Perhaps I should table insomnia as a defence for my actions, as a rationalization for the lion.

To be honest, I can't remember whether a horoscope advised me to buy a lion, whether my producer appeared in a dream and advised me to buy a lion, or whether, in a particularly troubled dream, I had been comforted by the sight of a man standing alongside his pet lion.

King of the Jungle

Because a hungry lion likes to eat meat, I bought a second refrigerator, and a large deep-freeze unit which I kept in the laundry. Most afternoons, the lion moped about in the back yard, but towards dinner time he began to paw at the kitchen door, making kitten noises that soon matured into deep-throated growls.

At one stage, I had it in mind to buy a micro-wave oven, but the lion seemed to prefer raw meat: steak, or failing that, hamburger mince. My butcher suggested that I try beef olives, but beef olives didn't agree with the lion. The big cat had an unsophisticated palate, which was probably as it should be. Having purchased the lion, I seldom ate out, and began to live pretty much as I had done when I was a schoolboy sharing the house with my parents.

Near Dark

Only when I'd been with the lion for several weeks did I remember a picture book given to me by my mother on my fifth birthday. The title, so far as I could recall, was *A Boy and His Lion*. I remembered that the predominantly black hardcover of the book featured a picture of a small redheaded boy walking with his pet lion.

The boy in the story is given a lion, or imagines that he has been given one, in order to help him to overcome his fear of the dark. Now it occurs to me that my mother must have chosen this book because I was afraid of the dark.

Or, more precisely, she bought the book because I was afraid of what might take place in the dark.

The Accessory

Old Mrs Davis in number eleven remembered when my mother walked the family's red cocker spaniel every night before tea. Passchendaele Street used to be full of kind old ladies who would stop Mum for a chat. Whenever Mrs Davis saw me walking the lion, she would call out, asking whether I had named the lion.

At one time, I'd considered giving the beast an ironic name like Wayne, Kevin, or Jason. Then I remembered my distaste for the pisspot enthusiasm of drunken fathers who name their boys after victorious cricket teams. I figured that being a lion was enough, that a lion could stand tall without a name.

Before the lion moved in, Mrs Davis would call out to me, Richard, when are you going to get married?, or, Richard, have you got yourself a girl yet? My few relationships had been short and disastrous, and I found it difficult to respond to Mrs Davis' personal inquisitions. Often I'd take the long way home just to avoid her. At other times, I faked nonchalance, Ah no, Mrs D, I'm still hunting for Miss Right, or, No, I guess the girls just don't know what they're missing out on.

The thing is, most of the girls did know what they were missing out on, and didn't consider that they were actually missing out.

I really had hoped that consorting with a great beast would increase my virility and make me more attractive to women. My knowledge of history indicated that sexual desirability is linked to fashion by way of innovative erotic conjunctions. Owning a lion would make me more distinctive. I always expected that my lion would make things happen.

When I told my friend Yuri that I intended to buy a lion, he argued that I was being transparent. Yuri said that I would be better off running some gel through my hair and buying a red BMW, as he had done.

Mate, you can't go making a dickhead out of yourself just because of Tracey.

Yuri suggested that Tracey would say that I was suffering from a rare form of 'conceptual dyslexia', a condition that leads men to confuse the idea of being alone with the idea of buying a lion.

Disregarding all real and imagined oppositions, I went to the pet shop that afternoon, and later, in a fever of newfound confidence, I bought a bumper sticker for my Datsun:

LOVE ME, LOVE MY LION

A Style of Compensation

In his early days as a stand-up comic, Woody Allen used to joke about his neurotic desire to return to the womb . . . *Anyone's* womb! That sort of allusion to oral sex must have been very risqué in the early 1960s.

Following the lead of my schoolfriends, I used to describe the act of cunnilingus as 'going the growl'. I suppose that the act became known as growling due to the noises emitted by the growler as he or she struggles to breathe with their face pressed tight into the woman's underside. I never considered that the term was in any way connected with lions or growling beasts, unless the person who coined the phrase had confused a lion with a loin.

As a young man, I discovered that you can only disappoint a woman so often, and, in the days before the lion, in the days when I was too often unable to pleasure a girlfriend by more conventional means, I made a serious effort to become adept at growling.

I vividly remember the first time, growling for Tracey in her bedroom, both naked under a veil of her undispersed cigarette smoke. There was music playing on her tape recorder, *Faith* by The Cure, one of those morbid dirges fashionable at the time. I must have growled for twenty minutes, to no obvious pleasurable effect.

I'm ready now, Tracey said, her fingers stroking the crown of my head, coaxing me to assume a copulative position.

As I shifted from the task at hand, I knew that I wasn't ready, and she saw that I wasn't ready. It also seemed that she had been unimpressed by my efforts to compensate.

Actually, I've been ready for some time, Tracey said.

What can a man do in these circumstances? I tried to sound apologetic. It doesn't look like it's going to happen, I said.

No, she said pointedly.

She moved away, pulling together the two sides of her black kimono.

At least you can't accuse me of being an opportunist, I said.

No. No one can accuse you of that, Tracey said, as she left the room to fix herself an omelette.

As I lay flat on my back, I gazed down at my ineffective genitals. From that angle, they looked to me like a small rocky outcrop in the grasslands, a portion of wilderness awaiting the arrival of a great beast.

Reading Between the Lions

Opening my letterbox one afternoon, I found no mail, just a folded note. The page carried a type-written message:

> WHAT HAVE YOU BEEN DOING
> WITH OUR CHILDREN?

After considering the note for a moment or two, I tore it up, having chosen to treat it as a juvenile prank. When several more notes— all carrying the same message— arrived during the following days, I thought about calling the police. It's some measure of the way that I was thinking then that I could persuade myself that these notes must be the work of the producer who had commissioned me to adapt *Approximate Life*. I was inhabiting a reality where these notes became a frustrated producer's way of telling me to get on with it.

The Lion Sleeps Tonight

I cleaned out the dining room so that the lion would have a room of its own, but the lion chose to sleep at the foot of my bed. The lion could be restless in his sleep, growling at dream natives, or clawing at the wall. To begin with, the intimacy of this sleeping arrangement gave me concern. I was scared of the time when my big cat would start to moult.

I've had a long history of allergic reactions to cat hair. When my face comes into contact with cat hair, my eyes puff up and my nose runs like a nasal Ben Johnson. I've had similar experiences when I've slept with smokers. Even if the woman wasn't actually smoking, the traces of stale smoke in her hair, or in her room, were enough to set me off. I still consider that nothing dulls passion more than a runny nose, and at that time I was sincere in the belief that my sexual potency with Tracey had been damaged by a constant fear that I was about to sneeze, or that my nose would dribble onto her face during lovemaking. I suppose that I wanted to believe that Tracey's smoking had inhibited my virility.

I anticipated that sharing a room with a lion would be not much different than sleeping with a smoker, but I was wrong. The lion's discarded hair never bothered me. So when people asked me about the disadvantages of owning a pet lion, I could see none.

If I'd ever paused to listen, I might have heard the distant beat of tom-toms in the jungle.

The Presumption of Guilt

My family had moved into Passchendaele Street, Hampton on the day that John F Kennedy was assassinated. I was three at the time.

In those days, Hampton was a quiet, friendly suburb inhabited by Great War veterans who lived in streets named after battles in the Great War. You can imagine what comfort it must have been to the shell-shocked survivors of Passchendaele to return to new homes in a street named after the Battle of Passchendaele. Years later, when I moved back to Passchendaele Street, only the nonagenarians like Mrs Davis knew me, and the complexion of Hampton had altered.

Where once there used to be second-hand Holdens and Volkswagens in Hampton driveways, there were now Volvos and BMWs. Most of the modest Californian Bungalows had been extended and renovated, and the high school opposite my home was forced to close when the suburb's affluent new residents chose to send their children to expensive private schools. As I walked the lion through the new Hampton, I felt that I was walking through an unsettled transitional version of the suburb I grew up in.

I suppose that I have always wanted to consider myself removed from petty matters of status. Only as a lion owner did I see how grotesque people become when their lives are ruled by envy and material acquisition. In this new, competitive Hampton, it soon became apparent that eccentricities of style bred resentment.

Pseudonymous letters began to appear in *The Hampton Bugle*, signed by Indignant and Concerned Ratepayer. The authors complained that the ownership of a pet lion contravened council by-law 14.6, that the local children were terrified of playing outside, and that neighbourhood pets were 'known to have gone missing'.

By the time these letters evolved into a petition, vicious lies had begun to circulate about the mysterious disappearance of two fourteen-year-old girls said to have been squatting in the derelict high school buildings.

Richard, have you signed the petition? Mrs Davis asked discreetly.

No, I haven't seen any petition.

It's to get rid of the child molester, she whispered.

Oh, I see. I'll have to keep an eye out for it then, I told her.

Not the Shadow of a Doubt

My friend Yuri runs a photographic studio in Hampton

Village, not far from the pet shop where I bought the lion. Yuri makes a substantial income photographing food for women's magazines. Though his photographs of blueberry cheesecake and pavlova are said to be world class, Yuri still dreams of establishing himself as a serious artist.

You've heard about this petition? I asked, as he led me into his darkroom.

Sure. It stinks.

What I really wanted to know was whether he'd help me to finance a defamation action.

Mate, Yuri said, sliding a sheet of paper into a tray of solution. Mate, face it, it's not a question of justice or decency. They hate you for having a lion.

So, what are you saying, that I should just cave in to these yuppie extortionists?

When he turned on the safe light, Yuri's face took on the same paternal expression as when he gave me my first packet of condoms.

Dick, lions don't suit you. Look at yourself. You're not a lion person. Seeing you with a lion disturbs people.

I couldn't believe that he'd reduced the issue to a matter of aesthetics.

No, listen, it offends them. They see you with a lion and it offends their idea that life should always be ordinary and regular and tasteful. When they see you with your lion . . . For them it's like seeing a man with a boner tearing a hole through his trousers . . . Hey, it might be different if you were a married man, I dunno.

You might say that Yuri was very perceptive, but I couldn't appreciate that at the time. I was unable to think clearly, or with any level of objectivity. I believed that my oldest friend had sided with my upwardly mobile enemies.

While Yuri fished about in the tank, I pulled a black-and-white photograph out of the drying cabinet. It had as its subject a man who had been photographed from an odd angle.

Who is this? I asked.

Oh him, Yuri said. He took the photograph and directed me to a stack of prints. It's one of a sequence, a conceptual series about a man who casts the shadow of a rat. No matter where he stands in relation to the light source, he casts the shadow of a rat. The critics call it Theoretical Expressionism. Took ages to set up.

I flicked through Yuri's photos. They were beautifully composed shots, and, in each, a slightly rotund man cast a rat-shaped shadow. Sometimes it was a fat rat, sometimes it was a long, skinny rat.

All that I could think to tell Yuri was that he was totally fucked in the head.

If the rat fits . . . Yuri said, smiling.

I smiled too, until I saw that Yuri was looking beyond me to the point where my shadow hit the wall. I refused to turn around.

Lyin' Mongrels

When the next note arrived, I finally saw that I had been deluding myself. I knew that my Hampton neighbours would be prepared to do anything, say anything, to get rid of me and the lion.

JUST STOP FUCKING WITH OUR KIDS!

Clawmarks

The house at 19 Passchendaele Street was bought at auction by a youngish couple, Greg and Louise Fleming. He is an actuary, and she teaches accountancy. The Flemings have two school-aged children, James and Penny, who they will send to St Leonard's College. Though the Fleming kids were fascinated by the clawmarks on the kitchen door, I could see that their parents had no interest in the history of the home or its place in the history of Hampton. The Flemings intended to extend and renovate.

After donating my lion to Melbourne Zoo, it was pointless for me to stay in a big house with a garden that needed looking after, so I bought a two-bedroom townhouse in St Kilda, in the hope of putting the lion and the irrational behaviour it provoked behind me. For a time, I entertained the notion of buying a second-hand BMW, knowing that friends would regard this as a sign of my return to wellness. Even without a high status vehicle, they embraced me as someone who'd managed to free himself from the grasp of a religious cult.

They might have thought differently if they had known how I came to put things into perspective. Or, should I say, how I came to put things into their perspective.

Those last few days were a blur, my fury mixed with rare anxiety, the lion going out of his way to be cute and indispensable, the impossibility of making a decision. Though I didn't tell anyone this at the time, a horoscope finally made the decision for me.

On October fifth, the entry under GEMINI read,

Because you have never been so appreciated, you have nothing to lose but appreciation. Now is not the time to linger or hesitate.

I don't know where in that I recognised myself, or saw the instruction *Get rid of the lion!*, but I was convinced that the message pertained to me only, and that *Get rid of the lion!* was what it said. How could I fail to act when I was receiving counsel that was so obviously uncanny? That's it, I said, you've got to sell the lion, or donate it, or do anything to delionize yourself.

And oddly enough, it was by acting on these bullshit extraterrestrial insights that I was able to satisfy my friends and detractors that I was as sane as they were.

Wombsickness

Yuri calls Melbourne The City of Dreams, by which he means that it's a city whose inhabitants dream of being anywhere but Melbourne.

I'm not so cynical. I'd prefer to dream Melbourne as it exists within my daydreams. If I could choose the content of my dreams in the same way that I might select a favourite movie on video, I'd dream myself a friendly suburb like Hampton once was, a Hampton where young men and women walk hand in hand through soft autumn sunlight, keeping pace with a lion who tugs at the leash when it catches the scent of cocker spaniel. I'm sure that it would ease my sense of indiscretion to have history rewritten to locate me as a man ahead of his time.

But the dreams I have are much less comforting. In the dream which recurs most frequently, I find myself driving through Hampton late on a warm night. It may be that I am expecting to find the lion, that I believe the lion to be lost. The Hampton streets seem unusually quiet. Unusually dark.

I turn into Passchendaele Street automatically, as I have done thousands of times. It's only when I see the Flemings' Volvo in the driveway at number nineteen that I remember the shift. I laugh at my absent-mindedness, but my amusement turns to unease when I am unable to remember my new address.

I sit in my car for a time, hoping that my head will clear, that my memory will return. If it was earlier in the evening, I could ask the Flemings whether they have any mail to pass on, and in that way I could get them to divulge my new address without embarrassment.

My chest pounds. I can't decide what to do. I get out of the car to grab some fresh air. After the steaminess of the day, I can smell the salt on the sea-breeze, and I would be calmed by the familiarity of this breeze if I wasn't overwhelmed by the sense that I am about to be seized by the darkness, that I'm going to be swallowed whole by the darkness.

And that's where my dream always ends, with me alone, enveloped by the darkness. I wake up frustrated and distressed. Yet, much as I might like to follow the truth of this dream through to its resolution, I fancy that it's one of those circles designed to be tauntingly incomplete. My challenge is to come to terms with its inconclusiveness.

I suspect that's why I needed to make this confession about my lion. I needed to place myself inside the histories that I once wanted to distance myself from; the history of ironies and foolishness, the history of sexual misadventure.

I'm still far from comfortable with my role in that larger story, but I now feel that I could look you in the eye when I admit that I was once, for six months in 1990, the owner of a pet lion, that I once bought a lion to compensate for an inability to express my sexual and emotional needs. Would it have been so different to have bought a red BMW?

Buying that lion was the only impetuous thing I'd ever done. Sure, my aspirations were unreal, and the pride I felt then was misplaced, but the debacle has helped me to understand the necessity of failure and embarrassment. You can't let yourself be intimidated by imperfection and uncertainty. You can't bury yourself away because you're scared of your own darkness. If I'm still embarrassed by my folly, I'm only embarrassed that few of my indiscretions have been so gloriously indiscreet.

The correspondence school

May 4

Sarah,

> once again you have displayed admirable style and
> technique. Your evocation of time and place is especially
> convincing. However, I can only give this piece a C,
> since you have responded with a work of imagination
> when you were instructed to submit an essay written in
> a personal (non-fictional) style. The Board guidelines
> are very rigid in this matter, and I refer you to p.31 of
> the Handbook. However skilled you may be as a
> creative writer, you mustn't imagine that your skills
> entitle you to operate outside the brief. If you resubmit
> by May 15, I will consider an upgrade of no more than
> ten per cent.

May 8th

Mr Thompson, I was very disappointed by the comments
(and mark!) on my recent story. I followed the instructions
you supplied and wrote a highly personal essay—rather
more personal than I usually present to strangers. Why did

you offer no specific comment about the content of my essay? You are very wrong to *presume* that it is a work of imagination. It may be that my suffering threatens or discomforts you in some way. I certainly will not re-write or re-submit till you are more precise in stating your objections to my story.

May 11

Sarah,

following your correspondence of May 8, I re-read your story 'Koorook', and I remain of the opinion that it is a (not inconsiderable) work of imagination. I should put my cards on the table: I know Koorook quite well. I lived there for the first three years of my life. My parents left Koorook for Melbourne on the day that John F. Kennedy was assassinated. I still have friends and relatives who live in the area. So far as I am aware, Koorook is not a stopping-off point for alien spacecraft. You say that the alien visitor from Zon-X closely resembled a Gas and Fuel plumber who once visited your house. If, as I suspect, you are writing a form of expressionistic autobiography, I think you need to be more cogent or telling in the parallels that you draw. Wild leaps of imagination diminish the credibility of your story. For instance, it's not obvious to me why your mother would 'slut off with' an alien simply because he shows an interest in her craftwork, and shares her taste for Belgian chocolate. Nor am I convinced that knowledge of such a liaison— is it sexual or merely intimate?— would disturb your 'father' to the extent that he would explore hitherto latent homosexual desires. If your story is to be construed as an innovative form of non-fiction, you need to make it apparent how these

115

metaphors operate as metaphors. As a reader, I need to have some cues which would enable me to decode or intepret your narrative. That said, even if you could persuade me that your mother's relationship with Gorb expresses a manifest yearning in her life, or that your father's misadventures after the football club Pie Night are the direct consequence of his failure to understand your mother's needs as you perceive them, I would still be inclined to say that 'Koorook' is a work of fiction. As such, it contravenes the specific guidelines for the second common assessment task set down in the Handbook. I am prepared to extend your re-submission deadlines to May 22, which would mean that it should be forwarded alongside your essay on The Go Between.

May 15th

Mr Thompson, it seems to me that Koorook must have changed quite a bit since you lived here. Whether or not you believe in a alien visitation doesn't really bother me. I know the truth, and I am looking forward to having Gorb's child. (I'm not so thrilled about having to tell my mother that we share a lover.) I would ask you to be more discreet in the notes that you attach to my essays. My parents often ask to read them. My mother is unaware that my father knows of her affair. Nor does she know that he has sought solace with the junior football coach. I don't understand what you mean about 'expressionistic autobiography'. I write about my life as I experience it. I don't know how I could write more personally or truthfully. For me, the only real truth is emotional truth. After all, if my memory of a dream or a desire is more compelling than my memory of an actual experience, how can I say that one is more 'real' than the other? By giving reality to my most truthful dreams and fears and desires, I am inventing a more real, more compelling version of myself. What could be more fictitious than the idea of a personality that is whole, discrete, and continuous? I would insist on getting a second marker, but it makes no difference now. I am going to have Gorb's child, and any academic ambitions I had are now secondary . . . I enclose my essay on *The Go Between*. Actually, I ended up liking the book quite a lot. Marion's situation—getting duffed-up by rustic Ted—isn't so different from my own. (Would you be my go-between, Mr Thompson? Would you help me if my father insists on an abortion?)

May 18

Sarah,

> *this is a fine essay. You write with great sensitivity about Leo's predicament, and the multi-dimensional aspects of moral decision making. I particularly enjoy your illuminating discussion re Hartley's use of cricket metaphors. This is definitely worth a High Distinction.*

May 24th

Mr Thompson, pleased as I was to get a high grade on my *Go Between* essay, I was disappointed by your lack of care or compassion. Since Gorb and his colleagues left for Zon-X, my mother has been stuffing herself with sedatives. She refused to believe that I'd had sex with Gorb until I described the mustard-coloured rings around his engorged penis. She hardly knows whether to smack me or beg me to forgive her. My father goes off into the garage with his stick-mags. He pretends that none of this has happened, but he'll piss off on us as soon as he's found work in the city. He has asked a specialist friend in Bendigo to 'attend to my problem'. I am dreadfully confused. I want my baby. Why have you chosen to ignore the matter entirely? Are you so frightened of being touched by reality?

May 27

Sarah,

> *I don't think you realize how busy I am. I process more than fifty pieces of student correspondence every day. I simply don't have the time or energy to buy into your fantasies. You are an exceptional student, and it is always a great pleasure to read your work. (Unfortunately, I'm not a great fan of science fiction.) With the job market the way it is at present, every mark will be crucial to your future prospects. Please don't waste this opportunity. You have a rare talent, but talent alone doesn't count for much. I'll expect your* Sons and Lovers *essay on June 5.*

June 2nd

Mr Thompson, last Thursday my father forced me to have Gorb's child aborted. He drove me to an expensive clinic in Bendigo, where a thin acne-scarred man, Dr Pascoe, sat me down and told me that I mustn't be ashamed. He said that country girls tend to be adventurous, and that these sort of mistakes happen as a matter of course. Dr Pascoe wanted to know who the father was, and whether I had his permission to abort. When I told him that Gorb was several light-years away and unable to be contacted, Dr Pascoe sneered and told his nurse that I was a smartarse. But when their vacuum began to suck out bits of crusty green foetus, he and his nurse were sick all over the place. Total gut panic. I was still under a local, and it was all I could do to calm them down. I shouldn't have expected anyone to understand. I was probably too hard on you. You could never understand. It was a ninety minute drive back to Koorook. There was a big squall and the rain belted against the screen so that the wipers could barely keep up, and all my father could think to say to me was, 'You know what you are, don't you?' My mother doesn't speak. I haven't been good for much these past few days. I've got a folio deadline for Australian History. I hope you'll understand if my *Sons and Lovers* essay is a couple of days late.

June 4

Sarah,

> *this has to stop!* *You're spending more time fabricating these bizarre diversions than you are on doing your work. Really, you seem to forget that I have information about you and your family on file. I know about your mother, Sarah. It's a terribly sad thing, but you can't go through life playing on people's sympathies. It doesn't do you any credit to concoct these stories about your father, or to make black jokes about abortion. Actually, I've had enough of this alien business. I expect to see your* Sons and Lovers *essay by June 11, or I'll be required to deduct marks.*

June 8th

Mr Thompson, so you know about my mother, do you? Who are you to say that you know about my mother, or that you know anything about my life? Do you really believe the lies my father told for your shitty files? He's never told the truth in his life. You say you know Koorook, you *know* about my mother. What you know is FUCK ALL! Since you know so much, maybe you should tell me what you're doing working at The Correspondence School. I've heard that The Correspondence School is a sheltered workshop for damaged teachers, all the worst basket cases. (I might have something about you here in my files. Let me see . . . Ah yes, your mother. Don't think that I don't know about your mother, Mr Thompson!) So what happened to you? Did a class of boys gag you, and gaffer-tape you to the ceiling? Maybe you just dropped the chalk one day and stood there bawling your eyes out. Or else you went home early to find your wife giving a slippery bit of private tuition to one of your star Lit. students. Just what are you doing there in that Ivory Cellar of yours? How can you presume superiority when you're so obviously Mr Fucked Up? (Just for your records, Mr Thompson, it *was* an abortion. You see, people have them . . . No, *girls* have them, out here in the real world.)

June 12

Sarah,

Once again this is a very fine essay that deserves an A. The observations that you make about Paul Morel and his inability to form mature relationships are very insightful. You would have benefited from greater attention to detail when discussing Lawrence's use of sexual symbolism. (And I do like your observation that Lawrence's high-frequency repetition of the words dark, darkening, darkness etc., articulates a kind of emotional tunnel-vision. DH is the most emotion-conscious of authors.) Speaking of emotions, I shouldn't have written what I did in the last note. It was out of line, and I'm sorry. Let's forget about it, and get on with the business of getting you a high mark in November.

June 14th

Dear Mr Thompson,

My daughter Sarah has asked me to write to you with regard to the feedback she has been getting on her assignments and stories.

As you will have gathered, Sarah is an imaginative, highly strung girl. She has suffered a great deal since her mother's death, and is given to dark moods and flights of fantasy. I know that Sarah is talented, just as I am aware that she can be very callous and manipulative.

I hope that you will try to understand Sarah, and not allow her indiscretions to get under your skin. She needs your help, and she needs remarks on her submitted work that are less perfunctory than they have been in recent times.

Yours sincerely,

James Dickson

June 17

Sarah,

I take your point. I was absolutely wrong to comment on matters that I knew nothing about. Yes, I ought to have written more extensively on your Sons and Lovers *and* Go Between *essays. I suppose that I was troubled by your previous remarks and felt helpless . . . Are you all right? . . . If nothing else, you will have a long and glorious career as a swindler. (I doubt that your father*

*would write so formally, or that he would type a short,
personal request. I do know that he doesn't press quite
so hard when making his signature!) I should have
received your answers to* The French Lieutenant's
Woman *questions by June 24.*

June 21st

Mr Thompson, yes I am all right, thank you. It just gets so
fucking boring here. It's either videos, netball, the pub, the
Young Farmers, or else you make your own fun. I'm sure
you know the old saying, When things are crook in
Koorook, they're totally shithouse. I love *The French
Lieutenant's Woman.* It's wonderful. If there weren't books,
I'd go spare. Tell me the names of your favourite authors
. . . And I *would* like to know what you're doing at that
school. As for my father's signature, and my version of it,
personally, I don't see how you could tell the difference.
Calligraphy's one of my favourite things. Calligraphy and
sex . . . There were lights in the sky again last night.

June 28

Sarah,

    These TFLW *answers are excellent. You need to be this
detailed when writing your essays. Always draw the most
pertinent details from the text to support your arguments
. . . My favourite books? Too hard.* Dead Souls *by
Gogol,* Gulliver's Travels *by Swift,* Lolita *by Nabokov,*
Labyrinths *by Borges . . . Kundera, Alice Munro, Ian
McEwan, David Ireland, Eugene Ionesco, Beverley
Farmer . . . far too many to mention . . . As for the
school, you weren't that far wrong. The Correspondence
School is a sheltered workshop for storm-damaged*

122

teachers. I wasn't really cut out to be a classroom teacher,
and, after I finished my diploma, I'd decided to give the
profession a miss. But then I was offered a soft job in a
boy's school, teaching English and Lit. to clever (mostly),
well-motivated (mostly) boys. I thought that I'd landed
on my feet. They actually enjoyed Shakespeare, T.S. Eliot
and Lowell . . . Then one Sunday, one of my boys got
upset, got drunk, got a rifle, and sat himself on a roof.
He shot some people as they drove past, strangers, and
then he shot dead (he said 'picked off') the people who
went to help the people he'd already shot . . . Look, I
don't know. It might be just an excuse, these things are
complicated. A lot of other things were going on at the
time. Maybe my being here, with all the other
basket-cases, has nothing to do with the shooting business.
It's not such a bad job though. I've always liked writing
letters. I'm much better with people on paper.

July 2nd

Mr Thompson, you're so sorry for yourself! You need to
get out and have some fun. How old are you? Are you
married? Do something outrageous, get yourself a lover or
a pet lion. Anything . . . I enclose the creative piece,
'Approximate Life' for my folio.

July 6

Sarah,
This time you were instructed to write an imaginative
piece, and you have, indeed, responded with a
powerfully disturbing work of imaginative fiction. I find
it very difficult to comment on this story, or to predict
how the examiners would respond if you were to produce

123

a similar piece of work in the examination. The first criticism that I must make is that this story isn't sufficiently self-contained. Your stories tend to leak, one into another. Certain details concerning Gorb and his motivations demand some knowledge of your previous (science) 'fictions'. The violence is too confronting. So is your use of coarse sexual language and imagery. I'm tempted to call your story pornographic, but I can hardly be dismissive when it is so imaginative, and when so much of what is currently revered as 'art' plays with these same sado-masochistic themes. I can understand why the alien Gorb might want to punish the narrator for aborting his child, but why does Gorb force her father to watch? The description of the father masturbating while Gorb rapes and brutalizes his daughter is too horrible to contemplate. I'm sure that you expect me to be shocked, and I am shocked. You would probably expect me to refer your story to a psychologist, but I don't think that I should allow you the pleasure of distraction, when distraction seems to be what you are after . . . Sarah, you mustn't take liberties with your talent. I'm going to give you an A here, in spite of my puzzlement and revulsion. I think you are capable of much better than this.

July 9th

Mr Thompson, *Revulsion*! You lousy hypocrite! First you bawl me out for playing games, then you write, 'I'm giving you an A here, in spite of my revulsion'. Who's living the fantasy now? I don't believe that you were revolted by my story. Otherwise, you would have shown it to a shrink. You might have been revolted by the fact that it excited you. I'm sure that an intelligent man like you would know about Freudian denial. I'm wise to you, Mr T. We're kindred spirits. I'm sure that we both enjoy the same games. Surely, you *must* have guessed who Gorb is by now?

July 14

Sarah,

ENOUGH!!! No more Gorb! No more juvenile games! I'm waiting for your essay on The Crucible. *I'll be required to deduct marks if it doesn't arrive by July 20.*

July 22

Sarah,

I haven't received any submissions since your correspondence on July 9. I'm also advised that you failed to submit folio work for Australian History. If I don't hear from you by the end of the week, I'll have to notify the Principal.

July 25th

Dear Mr Thompson,

Don't you think it's strange that a teacher would fail to notify the Department, or his superiors when a troubled girl submits a story about being raped and humiliated by an alien while her father watches and masturbates? Don't you think that it would be appropriate to bring that kind of thing to the attention of her parent? Why didn't you notify me when you suspected that my daughter had forged my signature? You worry me, Mr Thompson. What have you been playing at? Did Sarah's version of my signature look so different to this?

Yours sincerely

James Dickson

P.S. It's my guess that you knew who Gorb was all along.

July 27

Mr Dickson,

What have you done with Sarah? Why haven't I heard from her? Don't think that you can faze me with insinuated threats. I want proof that Sarah's all right. Otherwise, I'll have to question the police in Koorook.

Yours,
Richard Thompson

July 28

Sarah,

I'm very worried. Please contact me. If it's your father, we can help you. We'll do everything that we can.

July 31st

Mr Thompson, 'Sarah'? Really, you disappoint me. Still, it confirms what I've always heard, The Correspondence School is a sheltered workshop for damaged teachers, the last refuge for all the chronic basket-cases. Sure, come up and visit me here, by all means. Sgt Watson could use a giggle, and guys like you need to get out and have some fun. Twenty years ago, I had a fabulous English teacher down there at The Correspondence School, Mrs Corcoran. She only gave me 74 for the same *Sons and Lovers* essay that you went apeshit over. Have standards dropped that much? Your standards couldn't drop any further, could they? There are too many lights in your night sky, Mr Thompson. Too much perversity, and not enough honest to goodness, fun. Don't fret, Dick, 'Sarah' still sends you her wettest kisses.

Yours etc.

James

The Viennese scholar

Fathers and Sons

At the beginning of *The Great Gatsby*, Fitzgerald's narrator recalls his father advising him to beware of criticizing people, because few people were as advantaged in life as Nick Carraway had been. This was a period in American fiction when fathers used to give lots of fatherly advice. William Faulkner's great novel *The Sound and The Fury* becomes coherent at the beginning of the second section, when Quentin Compson recalls being given a watch by his father, along with the advice that he should use the watch not to remember time, but to remember the futility of trying to conquer time.

So far as I recall, Dad has never offered me philosophical advice of the kind that I could begin a great novel with. I think of my father as a peculiarly happy man, as gentle and good-natured as anyone you could meet, and I would have treated his advice with respect. But my father thinks like a scientist, and I'm sure that he figures that I can work things out for myself. So, in the modern way of inverting things, this story begins with a very specific piece of advice that I gave to my father. It takes a certain dickheadedness to offer advice to someone so in touch with the world as Dad, but I can be cocky, and besides, I stand by the advice that I gave him. What I said was that he should beware of Joseph Pauli.

My Father was a Teenage Expressionist

Though my sister Eliena is nineteen years old, she looks much younger, and with her black hair cut short, she could pass for fifteen. This childlikeness sometimes makes it difficult to take Lenni seriously. I was writing when she pushed open my bedroom door.

Whose room is he going to have?

Whose room is *who* going to have?

The Austrian student, Joseph Someoneorother. He wrote to Dad . . . Turns out that one of Dad's teachers at Grammar was a famous artist, and this bod from Austria wants to interview Dad for his PhD.

Because no one tells me anything, no one had told me that I was likely to be uprooted to accommodate a foreign guest. I tried to straighten things out with my parents while they were reading in the lounge.

Ah yes, Herr Pauli, my father said, looking up over the rim of his glasses. He wants me to be a footnote in his thesis.

Dad passed me the letter in which Joseph Pauli introduced himself as a doctoral student at the Vienna Institute of Art. Pauli said that he was writing a thesis on the beginnings of the Bauhaus movement, and his researches indicated that my father had been taught by Frederik Berg. Before Berg fled Europe in the late thirties, he'd worked with Gropius, Klee, and Kandinsky at the forefront of the Bauhaus school. Pauli said that he would be coming to

Melbourne to further his researches, and that he would like to have the opportunity to discuss my father's recollections of Frederik Berg.

Yes, I spoke with this Pauli chap on the phone a night or two back, my father said. Sounded more like a Yank than an Austrian, but that's how it is in Europe now, I expect. He's going to stay here a couple of nights.

I found the whole picture very confusing. My father was a professor of physics, just a month or two away from retirement. Before he slipped into academia, he had been the number two man at Defence Sciences. He wasn't an artist. He didn't even paint our house.

Frederik Berg presented your father with the art prize at Grammar, my mother announced. Your father was a teenage expressionist, even before they'd invented teenagers.

I dabbled, my father said.

Mother was much less modest on his behalf. She said that Berg had given my father an original oil painting as first prize in the senior art exhibition. This Berg original was gathering dust somewhere in the garage.

It's probably worth a fortune now, my father said, but it's a God-awful thing. Trees in blue and black. I prefer the really abstract stuff. I'm more of a Rothko man.

Meeting me must have stifled your father's creativity, my mother said as she lit a cigarette.

What about this man Berg?

Very decent chap, Dad said. Stiff, but knowledgeable.

He's dead now?

Yes . . . Well, he must be, my father said, considering the matter and making some mental calculations. Yes . . . Heard nothing of him for years, and he'd be kicking on for ninety at least. He must have died.

That night, I did a few mental calculations of my own. I thought about my father, and his relationship to Frederik Berg and Joseph Pauli. I was puzzled about what information the Austrian student could expect to get from my father, information that might be useful enough for Pauli to justify the expense of flying down from Canberra, where he had been studying the collection of Berg paintings held by the National Gallery.

I'm always the first person to admit that I have an overdeveloped imagination, but as I lay awake in my bed my mind ran wild with speculations:

1   Pauli knew of my father's Berg painting and wanted to steal it.

2   Pauli wanted to trick my father into selling the painting at a steal.

3   Frederik Berg had been a Nazi, or a Nazi spy, and Pauli was a Jewish Nazi-hunter seeking out Berg, or information concerning his associates.

4   Berg was a Jew or a Communist, maybe both, involved in a network of ex-patriot Austrians opposed to the Nazis, and Pauli was a new-model fascist trying to track down and discredit prominent anti-Nazis.

When I put these speculations to the family over breakfast, Eliena looked at me as if I'd been dropping acid.

All I was trying to tell them was that my father should be careful about what information he gave to this stranger, that Pauli's motives might not be scholarly.

I think that you're finding it difficult to accept that your father was a talented artist, my mother said, crunching her toast. You mustn't think that you possess the only creative mind in the family.

Someone has to question these things, I said.

Someone has to be an idiot to remind us what sanity means, my sister added.

Just you wait and see, I told them. This Pauli bloke will be bad news.

Mother always has the last word. Oh, for goodness sake, Richard. You're carrying on like the witch scene from *Macbeth*.

The Distractions of Youth

I had been out at a production meeting when Joseph Pauli arrived. Eliena met me at the front door. She was highly excited, whispering so that she couldn't be heard in the family room.

He has a friend with him . . . a *woman* friend.

I couldn't see why Lenni was making such a fuss about it. I put down my briefcase in the hall, and opened the door to the family room, where I saw Joseph Pauli sitting alongside my father as they looked over old photographs set out on the breakfast table. They turned as I entered, my father rising to introduce me, quickly followed by the scholar from Vienna.

Pleased to meet you, Richard, Joseph said as he leant forward to shake my hand.

I was surprised to find that he was a man of my age, only twenty-three or twenty-four, but very formally dressed in a black suit, white shirt, and sky blue tie. He had narrow cheeks, and circular glasses that rested on a long, thin nose. His jet black hair was greased, and combed straight back, so that he might have stepped out of a Christopher Isherwood novel.

Of course, you've already met my daughter, Eliena, Dad continued.

Ah yes. It's a very unusual name, Eliena, the Austrian observed.

Dad's fond of the Russian classics, my sister told him. He learnt Russian so that he could read the great writers in the original. Eliena's a character from Turgenev.

Eliena is a very charming name, he said.

So, is Dad changing the course of thought on Frederik Berg? I asked.

We've only just started, but his recollections are very interesting.

I was about to ask him why Berg had chosen to come to Australia when our conversation was interrupted by my mother opening the sliding glass door that led into the back garden. Accompanying her was a tall blonde woman.

Oh, it's such a beautiful garden, the young woman enthused in slightly forced English. Joseph, you must see the garden with torchlight. We saw squirrels with thin, white tails.

Possums, my mother suggested.

Oh, I'm sorry, possums, the blonde woman corrected, blushing as if she had made a terrible error. Joseph, such beautiful possums.

Eva, my mother said, this is Richard. Eva is travelling with Joseph.

My eyes hadn't left Eva since she entered the room. This Eva was, in my estimation, a very run of the mill Teutonic goddess; high pink cheeks, sea-blue eyes, blonde curls that cascaded over her broad shoulders, and breasts that were unavoidably large, however much I tried not to gawp at them.

I understood then why Eliena had been so excited. She'd been trying to warn me about the dangers of flying too close to the sun.

Eva is an actress, Eliena told me. She and Joseph met at a theatre in Berlin.

Heidelberg actually, Joseph said.

Eva moved to take a seat next to Joseph. The two of them made an odd couple; Joseph so measured, and Eva vivacious, bursting with energy, and very nearly bursting out of her white blouse. I couldn't imagine how a poseur like Joseph had managed to win Eva's heart. Joseph reached inside his coat to produce a very old-fashioned silver cigarette case.

What do you do, Richard? Eva asked.

I'm a television writer. I write comedy sketches for television.

That's wonderful, Eva said.

Television, Joseph said, pulling a cigarette out of the silver case.

We satirize politicians and institutions, I told them. It's not a great show, but it's better than most.

Yes, Joseph said, pausing to light his cigarette, I've seen television.

Joseph blew a thin trail of smoke out over the table and looked at me as if I was someone who had just confessed to molesting children.

Eva got up to assist my mother, who was pulling a roll of beef from the oven in the kitchen which adjoined the family room.

How was your flight from Europe, Joseph? Lenni asked. It's such a disgustingly long trip.

Oh, I slept, Joseph said.

It was a *fabulous* adventure, Eva said, with dramatic emphasis. I'd never flown before. And such a distance! You picture the earth and the oceans all spread out below you, and you know that down there people are shepherding goats, or going to banquets, or searching for food. They are learning to read, or wanting to cry.

While I sleep, Eva dreams, Joseph said.

No, you mustn't say it like that, she objected. You make out that there is something wrong with me for not ignoring things. When you fly, you fly over the whole tapestry of human experience. All the people down there who just then might be having their first kiss.

And all the men who make unnecessary trips to the dentist, my mother said as she stirred the gravy.

Yes, yes, Eva enthused. You fly over people who might be re-reading love letters. The millions of people who have never heard of Freud. A young girl hearing the piano for the first time. People who have never owned a toothbrush.

How about a couple who are just starting a relationship that will be the basis of a famous movie? Lenni asked, eager to keep the game in motion. Eva hardly needed encouragement.

People who look in the mirror and smile. People who look in the mirror and remember the fragrance of the breeze when they first fell in love. People who are too frightened to look in a mirror.

I looked at Eva, and imagined her imagining the ordinary miracles happening on the planet below her. It seemed to me that she wouldn't have needed jet engines to soar above the earth.

And Eva might have gone on, but she caught Joseph giving her a look which said, Enough. He was very thin-lipped then. He took another cigarette from his cigarette case and stood. I think I will look around your garden now, he said. To see your possums.

During dinner, Eva told the story of how she met Joseph.

She had been playing Kate in a travelling student production of *The Taming of the Shrew* . There was a scene in which Petruchio was to fling her to one side, but Eva hit a patch of water on the stage, skidded, and landed heavily in the front row of the audience.

She broke my nose, Joseph said.

With my elbow, Eva said, raising the elbow in question.

After the show, I went backstage to see how I would be compensated, Joseph continued.

And I decided that it would be cheaper to become his mistress, Eva said, beaming. And she placed her hand on Joseph's hand, and Joseph smiled for a moment, before pulling the hand away, so that he could return to his beef.

Since Joseph planned to spend the evening discussing Berg with Dad, Lenni suggested that she and I could take Eva to a movie in the city. I was thrilled when Eva agreed.

I parked the car some distance from the cinema, and as we walked through town we were caught in a sudden shower of rain. I cursed not having an umbrella, but Eva couldn't have been more delighted. She put one arm around my waist, and the other around Eliena. She pulled us close, and squealed with joy, pushing her face into the falling rain. How wonderful, she said. Spring rain in Melbourne.

We were caught up in Eva's joy, and the three of us danced and skipped our way to the cinema, drawing odd glares from other pedestrians. Eva insisted on holding our hands through the film, and she only released her grasp when she visited the toilet after the film ended.

What do you think of Joseph? I asked Lenni while Eva was gone.

He's cute. Sort of.

Cute! Austrians aren't ever *cute*! He looks like an anal retentive to me.

Cut the crap, Lenni said.

Yes, exactly. He's a crap-cutter.

And what do you think of Eva? Lenni asked me.

She's unbelievable. She's gorgeous.

I'm in love with her, Lenni declared, calmly.

Well, if you're going to chase after girls, I told her, you'd be wise to stick with girls from our planet. But how could I expect my sister to heed a warning I wouldn't have heeded myself?

It was an indelible evening. When Eva returned, she kissed each of us on the cheek, as if we were intimate friends that she hadn't seen for years. She was intoxicating. The smile only left Eva's face once, when we were driving home in the car.

Your father, he has beautiful eyes, Eva observed. So very bright. Artist's eyes.

They're scientist's eyes, I corrected. He's a physicist.

He used to work with the Defence Department, Eliena added. He did a lot of weird acoustic experiments. They were looking for ways to disable nuclear submarines.

A nuclear scientist! Eva said, horrified. Your father one of those criminals who would destroy the planet.

No, no, he was trying to disable nuclear submarines, I said. It was all theoretical. He's never even seen a submarine.

Hitler never visited the death camps either.

No, you're misunderstanding us, and it's all a non-issue anyway. Dad left Defence Sciences years ago.

There was a silence then, before Lenni changed the subject. Do you like Frederik Berg's paintings? she asked.

No, not much, Eva said, but I'm no fan of Bauhaus art. You'll have to ask Joseph about the paintings.

As it turned out, Joseph had already gone to bed when we got home at midnight. My father was drinking port, and looking over the Berg paraphernalia he'd shown to Joseph. I remembered the Berg painting when I saw it, and had to agree with Dad's view that it was a dreary thing.

So, are we sitting on a fortune? I asked.

Apparently not. It seems that I should have asked for one of Mr Berg's line drawings. Or one of his Kandinskys, even better.

Are they still in Australia, Berg's Kandinskys?

No, it turns out that he left for America in the fifties. I dare say that Peggy Guggenheim got her claws on them . . . You might be pleased to know that Frederik Berg died in 1970, in New York, so your speculations were off the mark.

But Dad didn't seem very pleased with his victory over my imagination. In fact, he looked quite disconsolate, and I began to think that something must have happened while we were gone.

Dad said that he hadn't been of much assistance to Joseph. He'd been able to suggest a couple of addresses, lend him some photos of Berg at Grammar, and that's all. He hadn't been able to remember anything worthy of a quotation.

I spent that night on the couch in the family room. It wouldn't be accurate to say that I slept there. I thought a lot about Eva and Joseph sharing my single bed, and about the warmth of Eva, her arm tight around my waist. I heard sharp, thumping noises, and imagined for a moment that it was Joseph fucking Eva in my bed, but it turned out to

be a couple of heavy-footed brushtails entertaining themselves on the roof.

It must have been after four when the fluorescent light
flicked on in the kitchen. I heard someone pour a glass of
water, then I saw Eva step back from the sink. She was
naked, but for a pair of skimpy white underpants, long
blonde hair falling over her magnificent breasts. She was
as startled to see me as I was to see her.

I'm so sorry. I didn't know you were sleeping here. I
thought there was another room.

She was much more embarrassed about having woken
me than she was about her nakedness.

It's all right, I said, my eyes tracking every quiver of her
breasts, I wasn't asleep anyway.

Eva came toward where I was on the couch, and just
for a moment I thought that reality and fantasy might be
about to merge.

Do you think that the world will end in a nuclear
holocaust? she asked me.

The question took me by surprise. I told her that I
am a pessimist in most things, that there might be a
catastrophe, but I didn't think that it would obliterate
everything. Somehow, life would go on mutating and regen-
erating, no matter what.

But our lives, the destruction of everything that we've
created and valued. Doesn't that matter? What would you
do to save human civilization? Would you kill yourself for
the sake of the earth?

I was caught off guard by the morbidity of Eva's inter-
rogation. If my wits had been working, I might have
reminded her that I am a comedy writer. Any comedy
writer would happily kill himself if he could be certain that
it would get a big laugh. But I stammered, and anyway,

Eva had her hand resting on my arm, so that the proximity of her nakedness was all that I could think of.

Never mind, she said.

Just at that moment, the door opened, and Joseph entered. He was wearing a pair of black jockey shorts. His dark hair was ruffled, and he was without his glasses. Joseph seemed remarkably unsurprised that Eva should have engaged me in conversation while being almost totally undressed.

Please forgive Eva, Joseph said. She wanders at night.

I was asking Richard what that noise was.

Just possums, brushtails, I said quickly.

When I came to next morning, it was well past eight, and the family was rattling breakfast plates around me. There was no sign of Joseph and Eva.

When do you think they'll get up? I asked. I need to get the computer from my room.

Joseph and Eva have already gone, Dad said. There was a phone call early this morning. Something urgent.

I hope you've checked to see that we still have our original Frederik Berg.

Don't let your imagination get in the way of the truth, Dad said.

I was only asking.

Don't be a fuckwit always, Lenni said. She was annoyed that she hadn't been able to say goodbye to Eva. I think that she wanted to tell Eva that she loved her.

A Dagger of the Mind

Though Eva still wanders in and out of my fantasies, I

haven't heard anything of Eva or Joseph since then. Dad said that Joseph promised to return the photographs and send him a copy of the book when it appeared, but of course, there was no guarantee that Joseph's thesis on Berg would be published. For a day or two after Joseph and Eva's departure, Berg's painting was given a place of prominence in the lounge. Then it was relegated to the garage. I'm sure it isn't a piece of work that Frederik Berg would want to be remembered by.

Unfortunately, we're not always remembered for our best works.

A short time after Joseph and Eva left, I came home to find a note to the effect that my parents had flown to Sydney, and would be away for three nights. One of Dad's old workmates had died, and they were taking the opportunity to catch up with some Sydney friends after the funeral. I mightn't have thought any more about it if I hadn't seen a short item on that evening's news bulletin.

A man described as a senior public servant had been shot dead in his Mosman home some time on the previous weekend. Police believed that Peter Sandford had disturbed an intruder, but they hadn't yet ascertained whether anything had been stolen. The news report highlighted a black and white photograph of the victim shaking hands with the former Prime Minister, Gough Whitlam.

I remembered Peter Sandford very well. He had visited our home many times when he and my father worked together in Melbourne. He was a tall, affable man with a ruddy complexion. He loved to drink, and to tell stories about the politicians and dignitaries he had met. He was Dad's superior at Defence Sciences, and my father liked him very much, though he had often criticized Peter for being politically expedient.

It disturbed me that someone I'd known had died so

violently, and I knew that my father would be feeling Peter's death dreadfully. Lenni spoke to Mum on the phone the next afternoon. Mum was OK. Dad had got very drunk at Peter's wake. The two of them were staying with cousins at Crow's Nest.

Because a murder in Sydney is deemed to be Sydney news, there was no follow-up report on television that evening, but the radio bulletin reported the funeral of the murdered public servant, Peter Sandford, along with the news that Federal Police were wanting to speak to a young German couple who had met with Sandford on the evening of his death.

Now, I warned you earlier that I have an overdeveloped imagination.

My mind readily exaggerates things, sees motives and conspiracies that aren't there. My imagination often gets me into trouble. But I also make a reasonable income writing comedy sketches from the bizarre things that travel through my mind. While it's easy to disparage overcooked thought, you need to remember that the truth broadcasts on many different frequencies.

That said, I wasn't going to expose these new concerns to ridicule from Lenni or my mother, and I wasn't sure how I should raise them with my father.

Dad was very depressed when he got home. He said that it was a terrible thing for someone to die like that. Police told him that they were certain that it was a burglary, that they believed some cash was missing. Dad had spent most of the three days in Sydney drinking, and reminiscing about Peter, and he wanted me to keep him company through a whisky bottle. At the halfway mark, I asked him whether Peter had been doing classified work.

Not that I know of, Dad said. We don't have real secrets

any more. Just commercial secrets. Science is commerce these days.

Peter couldn't have been trading in information then?

A spy! Who on earth would he be spying for?

All that acoustic stuff. There are still submarines. I'm sure that someone could use it.

I asked Dad whether he and Peter were on the same side, expecting that the question would annoy him, but he was more unsettled than irritated, and chose to give an ambiguous answer.

I'm sure that we'd both say that we were on the right side.

I wasn't asking what side you thought you were on.

I was *always* on the right side.

Then I tossed him my googly. I told him that I didn't know that he and Peter had been at school together.

We weren't. Peter went to school in Adelaide. What gave you the idea that we were at school together?

I don't know. I just thought that he might have been another protege of Frederik Berg, that you and Peter might have been the teenage expressionists at Grammar. That the three of you might have been part of a circle.

Dad put his whisky glass down on the coffee table. We were both very drunk.

Look, I only know one thing for sure, my father said. The world's a complicated place. Best to steer clear of the complications that can't be uncomplicated. You hope that the truth will win out, but in the long run, you only end up believing what you want to believe.

Always steer clear of complications that can't be uncomplicated. Is that the fatherly advice to start a novel with, or has the world got too complicated for fatherly advice to be of any use?

Whether or not he takes his own advice, my father has always been an unusually happy man. He plays his old records by Tom Lehrer and Barry Humphries, and he can still recite his favourite passages from Gogol and Lermontov. He sings Gilbert and Sullivan in the shower. If I choose to believe in my father, it's not just because I want to believe in him. I need to believe in fixture, and a capital-G Goodness that goes beyond good intentions.

Let me ask you this, could anyone who believed that he was accomplice to an evil or treacherous act sing so wholeheartedly as my father sings under the shower?

The fiction consultant

I doubt that it is possible for someone who has never written fiction, or had a work of fiction rejected, to fully understand the heartbreak of watching a postman deliver to your address an envelope addressed in your own hand, when you know that the envelope contains a returned work of fiction. If I could distance myself from the experience, I might find a metaphor exact or telling enough to convey to non-writers the distress of that moment. The closest thing that comes to mind is being told by a teacher that one of your children will never amount to anything. But that won't do. The anguish of literary rejection is a very specific anguish.

It shouldn't surprise you that I don't recall any of those moments in detail. Literary rejection is the type of disappointment that you bury away in the least accessible folds of memory. The truth is not so much that I can't remember, but that I don't want to remember. I don't want to recall where I was when I opened the self-addressed envelope that contained the manuscript of *A Summer Festival of Kissing*. Nor do I wish to recall whether I stood or sat while I read the editor's polite note, and her fiction consultant's extensive comments. I do know that two months passed before I had my emotions sufficiently under control to be able to re-read the opening section of my rejected story.

THE KISS LIST

Ever since my first romantic kiss at the age of seventeen, I have recorded and filed all of my kisses on a numbered sequence of index cards, cross-referencing the kisses where necessary. With the introduction of my new kiss measurement formulation, enabling an expanded profile and analysis of the individual kiss, I may find it necessary to transfer my records onto a computer-based file. Even if this eventuates, I doubt that I will ever destroy the neatly written cards which detail my first, tentative explorations of the kiss.

My practical interest in kissing began during October in my final year at high school. Though Georgina Christianson was my friend Yuri's girlfriend, she used to laugh at my weak puns, and I fancied her with an intensity that was new to me. I had gone with Georgina to study at her house, but we had only walked halfway before we were caught in a sudden violent cloudburst. We began to run, Georgina grabbing my arm as we crossed the street, wanting to lead me to shelter on the veranda of a nearby home. I was shy about entering a stranger's property, so I steered her back under a large gum tree. The air was warm, and we were both ridiculously wet. Catching a hint in Georgina's eye, I pulled her to me, and we kissed as the rain bucketed down.

You can whistle and jeer as much as you like, roll Jaffas down the aisle, but I'm not going to apologize for the energetic incompetence of that first kiss, for the wet hair sticking to my forehead, or for the heart thumping at the back of my rib cage. That was the way that it happened.

In the card index it appears as

No. 1   Georgina CHRISTIANSON
May St. Hampton 12/10/77
Approx. 10 seconds
Slight dizzy sensation
Slight loss of feeling knee region
Strong tumescent reaction

The Fiction Consultant's comments at the end of this section informed me that my narrator's description of this first kiss, the kiss that I had always considered to be a precious moment of spontaneous desire, might be read as a clichéd episode betraying a debt to Hollywood cinema of the '40s and '50s.

If you didn't know that he was one of Australia's most important writers, you might say that Bernard O'Connell was a remarkably ordinary man who leads a life of dazzling mundanity. Far from being the Artist fired by uncontrollable creative passions, Bernard O'Connell is fixated with order and regularity. He is widely known as an author whose interest is to explore the very specific, specifically interior, dimensions of individuals who lead outwardly quiet suburban lives. Few readers would guess the extent to which Bernard O'Connell's life enacts his literary vision.

Except for an apparently deliberate inexactness when shaving the tuft of moustache beneath his nostrils, Bernard's life is based on precision. Each morning he rises at exactly 6.15 to commence a day divided into compartments and regimes. After making himself a cup of coffee, he will write for seventy-five minutes between 6.30 and 7.45. After breakfast, he drives his thirteen-year-old Corolla to the university, where his day is divided between lecturing on fiction, seeing students, and attending to the business of being a well-known literary figure. At exactly five-fifteen every evening, he picks up Kaye, the younger of his two daughters. She will be waiting for him outside a friend's house, where she spends the ninety minutes after finishing school. Bernard will dine with his family, and discuss matters with his wife, Annette, before retiring to his office at eight-thirty. Sometimes he types and corrects his morning's work. Mostly, he researches the form-guides, and familiarizes himself with racehorses, jockeys, and trainers. At weekends, Bernard takes whatever opportunity he can to attend race meetings at Flemington. He is, from what I've seen, a moderately unsuccessful gambler.

If you were to peer through the window into the O'Connells' kitchen, you might see Bernard eating in the way of a pleasure-postponer, always attending to his orange vegetables, green vegetables, roast potatoes, and meat in that order. This isn't to say that he is unaware of his eccentricities, or proud to be so fastidious. Quite the contrary. As a well-known author, Bernard is embarrassed that he feels compelled to act in a fashion that draws attention to himself. He is ashamed that he still fears that his life will collapse if he abandons his regimes. He knows that an obsessive fearfulness is unbecoming for a public figure recently turned fifty years of age.

In the past five years, Bernard has supplemented his income by acting as the Fiction Consultant to the prestigious intellectual journal *Approximate Life*. He takes these duties very seriously. Because he is keen to identify and encourage young literary talents, Bernard often returns manuscripts with as many notes written in green ink as there are typewritten words on the page. He is not unaware of the dangers in being so forthcoming. Even talented young writers tend to be sensitive to critical encouragements. Bernard often describes his position at the journal as the F . . . . . C. . ., because he imagines that's how many aspiring writers refer to him.

The mistake I made was to trust Bernard O'Connell's judgement. I wanted to believe that Bernard O'Connell would understand my work, because he knows what it is to cultivate a challenging, idiosyncratic style. I hoped that he would recognise me as a fellow traveller, a writer of distinctive vision. And I expected that Bernard O'Connell would recommend my story to the editor of *Approximate Life*. He did not.

I failed in my earlier attempt to communicate the shock of receiving my manuscript covered over in Bernard O'Connell's green scrawl. I know that this will sound overdramatic to those of you who haven't experienced rejection or acute disappointment, but I felt like Bernard O'Connell had dropped his trousers and defecated on my soul.

Had the criticisms come from anyone else but O'Connell, I would have written them off as the jealousy of an imperceptive hack and thought no more about it. After all, it's not as if you expect justice or recognition in such an uninspired climate. But Bernard O'Connell knows how lethal a green pen can be. It's well documented that you can kill a person with an ordinary biro. You can sneak into an adversary's room while they are sleeping, push the pen into their mouth, and shove it up through the soft palate at the back of the mouth so that it penetrates the base of the brain. Someone as conversant with the Australian literary scene as Bernard O'Connell would understand that the astute use of a green pen can kill off a rival even before that rivalry has been signalled.

My story, *A Summer Festival of Kissing* is a peculiar, disjointed narrative about my own obsession with kissing and the desire to kiss. It is a story about my lifelong determination to understand the allure of kissing. I don't believe in disguising the autobiographical centre of my narratives. I am even reluctant to call them fictions, though the stories incorporate attitudes and events that aren't factual. I prefer to believe that I am advancing a new form of prose called 'autobiographical expressionism', where outrageous distortions and extrapolations are used to communicate interior truths.

Any true version of a person's life would not discriminate between that person's actions, desires, dreams, memories, fears and fantasies by creating or presuming a hierarchy of importance. Such a version would not trade on a false opposition between the real and the imagined. I detest the word authenticity. So much autobiographical writing, or fictionalized autobiography, is strangled by its adherence to these absurd hierarchies. You can't tell me that consciousness is perfectly regular and compartmentalized. The moment you describe an experience as fantasy or daydream or phobia, the moment you fix it with a mundane term or cue, you give the reader licence to disregard its cogency, to treat it as something of lesser importance, as unreal or irrational. This despite the fact that our lives are lived as much in the past or future, or speculative pasts and futures, as they are in anything so 'concrete' or 'real' as the present moment.

I have given my own name, Richard Thompson, to the person who narrates my story. Thompson's narrative mingles personal anecdotes about the most crucial kisses and near kisses in his/my life with statements concerning his mock socio-scientific ambition to optimize the efficiency of the kiss as a form of human expression. He is determined to eliminate confusing or confusable kisses. Like me, he sees ambiguous kisses as a major source of human misunderstanding. My intention is to represent this extrapolated version of my search for understanding as no more bizarre than my troubled and confused personal experience of kissing.

Yet my shifts from hard reality to expressionistic invention seem to defy Bernard O'Connell's comprehension. The Fiction Consultant is particularly unhappy with my decision to have my first-person narrator travel under the same name as the story's author. Later, he goes on to dismiss a whole strand of my story with the pejorative 'whimsy'. Having closely observed Bernard O'Connell's behaviour, I find it difficult to imagine that he has ever been whimsical.

Why doesn't O'Connell realize that I have no choice in this matter? I am writing truthfully and honestly about myself, endeavouring to chart the sometimes ridiculous course taken by my consciousness. If my narratives are silly, unconvincing, and distracted by conventional terms it is precisely because I am seeking the truths contained by silliness, distraction, and avoidance in order to redefine the understanding of the essential, or truthful.

So much autobiographical writing is tokenistic in its inclusion of embarrassing desires or incidents in order to suggest the honesty and integrity of an author who can rise above conceit and embarrassment. I do not wish to rise above conceit and embarrassment. My life *is* its conceits and embarrassments. The sum of a life is not much more than ignorance, discarded certainties, and irony.

The fantasy or whimsy that Bernard O'Connell derides as 'froth' is central to my wider project of replacement myth. Because Richard Thompson cannot explain his passion for the banal, middle-class suburb of Hampton, he reconstitutes Hampton in a way that makes it possible to communicate those feelings. *A Summer Festival of Kissing* features the exaggerated operations of a scientific institution where Richard Thompson furthers his investigation into the kiss. Bernard O'Connell doesn't seem to think that you can exaggerate the world without wanting to use those exaggerations as the basis for a Swiftian satire on institutions or pseudo-sciences.

Why do I need to read about Thompson's work at the Doisneau Institute, and his comic book equations and formulations, when his memories, fears, and daydreams are so much more compelling?

The Fiction Consultant would have me dispense with Thompson's mock-theoretical enquiries. He suggests that I ought to construct a new story by cutting and pasting Thompson's recollection of crucial kisses, and elaborate the circumstances which reactivate those memories in his mind. The Fiction Consultant is encouraging me to gather my material into a readily comprehensible story of the kind that he would write, as if this version of my life could be turned into the kind of life that Bernard O'Connell would lead. He uses his ticks, asterisks, and circled asterisks to coax me to betray my vision. He tries to deflect me from my truths toward his.

AMBIGUOUS KISSES

Analyzing my career to this point, I would say that, of all the kisses I have experienced, one kiss from Francesca was most instrumental in determining that I would convert my fascination for kissing into a life of scientific enquiry.

Francesca and I kissed at Melbourne Airport when I was leaving to spend five months travelling through Europe. I had already shared farewell kisses with two other close friends, Catherine and Elizabeth, but the unexpected intensity of Francesca's kiss nearly persuaded me to tear up my ticket.

When does a pile become a heap? When does a farewell kiss become more than a farewell kiss? Are the elements which might redefine a friendly or chaste kiss as a passionate kiss capable of being isolated and quantified? I knew that if I could find a means of clarifying confusable kisses, I might be able to eradicate a major source of human tension.

During the five months that I travelled, my lips retraced the path of Francesca's disconcerting kiss, and my mind pursued the theoretical questions aroused by that kiss. I was thinking about Francesca's kiss as I stood at the base of Glastonbury Tor, remembering her kiss as I walked by the river Seine in flood, mentally recreating her kiss as I sipped Pilsener from a tall glass in a gloomy East Berlin bar. When I looked at the other men sitting alone in that bar, all peering into the gloom, I believed that each of them was trying to recapture the essence of a lost kiss.

Approximate Life's Fiction Consultant would have me speak to him only with truths that correspond to or ignite the half-formed truths in his own mind, truths that might open the door to emotions that he has been unable to articulate. What he doesn't want is for a writer to challenge his intelligence by insisting that he pursue the more difficult questions raised by the incongruities of my narrative. So it is to be expected that Bernard O'Connell would enjoy this discussion of Francesca's ambiguous kiss, because it calls to mind certain troubling kisses from his own past. He would argue that it is the business of true fiction to investigate the precise meaning of persistent memories in this way. In turn, I would argue that it is equally the business of literature to propose, prescribe, and redefine, to offer the truths within the unfamiliar quite as much as it is to offer the familiar made new.

I haven't been able to satisfy O'Connell that Thompson and I are psychologically indistinguishable, that Thompson's bizarre preoccupations are an exact equivalent of my own manias. The Fiction Consultant is determined to read my unhinged scientist as invention, fancifully distinct from the world his author knows most intimately. I can only suspect that Bernard needs to read Thompson this way because he is loathe to accept that such strangeness might inhabit the world he seeks to regiment.

My scientist is nothing more than the expressionistic projection of my own more unsettling impulses. If I could convince Bernard that the scientist Thompson's extreme obsessiveness is a fair approximation of my own, he would be forced to acknowledge the cogency of my artistic vision. When I re-read Bernard O'Connell's comments, I see him virtually demanding a demonstration of mental instability sufficient to prove that my truths are certifiable truths.

> *But he's* not *a scientist conducting research into kissing, is he?*
> *. . . These fanciful passages bring to mind the silly*
> *speculations of journalists trying to fill daily columns . . .*
> *This does not interest me.*

Why must he obsess about the authentic, or the convincing? I don't live in order to be convincing. I don't dream in order to become more authentic. As an autobiographical expressionist, I am not writing about who I ought to be, or the dreams or fears that I ought to have, but the ones that actually dictate my thoughts. I write from the multiple intersection of fear and desire, hope and disappointment, knowledge and uncertainty, memory and forgetting, optimism and pessimism, dream and reality. No point at that intersection is more crucial or authentic than any other.

Though Bernard O'Connell has often expressed his contempt for the seldom-challenged truths and jargon of psychoanalysis, he would have me bring a false coherence to my narrative by invoking the spirit of Freud. He wants me to look beyond the immediate so that I might offer the suggestion of suppressed or ulterior desire.

THE KISSES OF THE ENEMY ARE DEADLY

Sometimes, mid-kiss, I need to remind myself to suspend analysis of the situation. I typed a short statement which I keep blue-tacked to the wall above my bed, underneath my framed print of Edvard Munch's *Shriek!*

> **Relax. You are a kisser, not an air-traffic controller. No one will perish if the kiss goes wrong.**

I may decide to remove this statement. More often than not, it acts to remind me of a gratuitous observation made by Tracey's wonderfully indiscreet sister, Jellybean.

I can't even imagine you kissing a girl, Richard.
You've seen me kiss Tracey.

Oh! . . . Oh, is that what you call it? In that case, I'd keep the number of a dentist handy to the phone.

I tell myself to relax because I tend to worry about things that shouldn't concern me. Does it matter that it might not be perfect? Does it matter that I know more about kissing than I know about women? I don't imagine that Einstein or Rutherford knew any more about women than I do.

This section seems close to the real story. When I read these pages, the bits about the International Summit of Kissing in

Atlanta, and the formulas and ratios fall away like husks.
I've seldom read a story which has so insisted that I ask,
'Why do you need to write this story?' Surely, this is a story
about someone who is so preoccupied with kissing that he has
lost sight of the women he kisses, lost the natural connection
between kissing and fucking. I'm deeply interested in the
subjects of kissing and fucking, but your scientist is a passive
blockhead unworthy of the consideration you give him.

Bernard O'Connell can tell me that I am a blockhead, but
I'm not *just* a blockhead. He may find my use of mock-
science to be disingenuous, but I suspect that he is trans-
ferring his own feelings of evasion and disingenuousness
onto me.

Maybe the Fiction Consultant uses words like fuck and
fucking in front of his friends at the racetrack, but I'd like
to bet that he wouldn't use those words in front of his
parents, or his children's teachers. O'Connell doesn't want
to recognize that I am writing with unusual honesty, that
the deficiencies and limitations of my narrator are *my*
limitations. He is so keen to assess and dismiss my narrative in terms of competent or accomplished literary fiction
(according to his own narrow definition), that he is unable
to see that I am detailing the integral personality at the
point of its disintegration.

Would pretending to be other than what I am give my
narrative more truth or integrity? Would using the word *fuck*
when I mean *kiss* make my story more earthy, or more
readily comprehensible? The truly eccentric threatens our
sense of ourselves and our place in the *scheme*. I expected
Bernard O'Connell to understand that.

What gives the Fiction Consultant the right to place
asterisks against crucial episodes from my life and say that
they are unbelievable, or incredible, or contrived? Or even

to judge, as he does in the section *Vampire's Kiss*, that they are 'interesting'?

VAMPIRE'S KISS

In the film, *Vampire's Kiss*, the actor Nicolas Cage plays a disturbed publishing executive who forms the mistaken belief that he is a vampire, making life a misery for his temporary secretary. On his desk sits a framed portrait of Franz Kafka, and when my friend Gabriella saw this, she made an involuntary yell, 'Kafka!', much to the amusement of the audience in the Valhalla Cinema. Because Kafka's portrait is seldom seen in films, I consider it reasonable that a person might want to honour his appearance with a commemorative yell. When I saw *Vampire's Kiss* at another cinema nearly twelve months later, as many as a dozen people yelled 'Kafka!' when the portrait appeared, so the cult has acquired a following.

I saw quite a few vampire films in the company of Gabriella, who is the sister of my friend Yuri. Her pale, bloodless beauty always seemed to make the choice of a vampire film obvious enough. On one particular occasion, we were at Gabriella's house, watching Max Schreck star as the vampire in the silent classic *Nosferatu*. I'd been wanting to kiss the delicate Gabriella for some time, but we were both shy, and extremely conscious of my long friendship with her brother.

When the film finished, I contrived to sneak up on Gabriella as she reclined on the floor, placing a soft vampire bite on her neck. I might have feared a shriek, but Gabriella remained impassive. I advanced to her lips. Gabriella is a slender, mysterious girl, a subject stolen from Modigliani, but her lips were cold and unyielding.

What's the matter? Don't you want to kiss me?

It's not that. We've known each other since I was eleven. It would be like incest.

In that situation, what was the use of arguing that we had

no blood relation, and that incest is a legal prohibition, not a psychological one? Gabriella was a lost cause. However desirable, she was not a passionate person, and what passion she had was reserved for Kafka.

The Fiction Consultant's interest in this section is not his interest in my kiss, or my frustration, but his interest in Kafka. (Perhaps this explains why he gave his daughter a quaint, outdated name like Kaye.) Bernard O'Connell is just another reader drawn to cyphers and allusions.

But why did you need to write this story?

I needed to write a story about kissing because I cannot in my heart believe that there is anything more fascinating or urgent than the desire to kiss, or anything so painful as the frustrated desire to kiss.

I realize that my views are strange and extreme, but they are no more extreme or unpalatable than the impulse to contaminate a young writer's precious recollections with notions of 'interest', with indiscreetly expressed preference or indifference, or even to suggest, as O'Connell does in one instance, that my paradoxes are insufficiently paradoxical.

When you pass judgement on a work of autobiographical expressionism, you pass judgement on the veracity of the author's engagement with the world. Bernard O'Connell would like to believe that judgements of this kind are his entitlement.

What's to stop me reading this as the sort of story that I've told you earlier that I would like to read—the story about a solitary maniac, scribbling about an imaginary institute and remembered kisses? I assure you that I am not trying to do

more than report my honest reactions when I say that your
whimsical pretexts do not interest me.

This could hardly be more calculated. O'Connell is goading
me. He goads me by insisting that the only convincing
maniac is someone who lives and breathes mania.

I could campaign against Bernard's reputation. I could
subvert him. My surveillances have given me information
that would damage him at work, and within his family. But
I like to believe that he respects my imagination, that he
would expect more from me than second-rate subversion.
And Bernard deserves an imaginative response. After all,
he's stolen fragments of my memory, and contaminated
them with base jealousies. He's spoken to me as if I was
an idiot.

I have been foolish, but I'm not a fool. I was once foolish
enough to trust Bernard O'Connell with my precious
kisses, and he betrayed that trust. His only concern was to
rid himself of someone who might rise to challenge his
authority. His obvious malicious intent betrays his wariness.
And the Fiction Consultant is right to be wary.

You need to focus your energies, to strip away everything that
isn't vital . . . It's not enough to tell me about the urgency of
Thompson's quest, I need to experience that urgency . . .

Yes. A jaded critic needs to experience urgency.

Everything about Bernard O'Connell's life is predictable.
He drives down the same streets at the same time each
weekday. At 5.15 every evening, his young daughter Kaye
sits on the red fire hydrant cover outside number three
Sterling Street, and waits for her father to arrive. She puts
her arms around his neck. He smiles and gives her a chaste
kiss. Despite his absolute regularity, he asks if she has been

waiting long, and she always says, Too long, but in truth she never waits more than five minutes, and he would have her wait no longer than that because he knows of the many troubled people who live in a vast metropolis like Melbourne.

Steven Spielberg

*I*t seems to me that you're fixated with mysterious
external forces . . .

External forces?

That you feel as if you're not in control of your own destiny . . .

I used to believe that I could influence things, that if I
was imaginative enough I could create relationships, that
I could invent a version of the world where I could be
happy . . .

Used to?

Well . . . It goes back to when Catherine and I were in
partnership as literary agents. We were handling a dozen
or so writers, all topnotch, and we'd got involved with a
Californian producer, Ray Bennett. Ray was keen to buy
the options on some treatments that were kicking around
. . . It got touchy. We thought that we were dealing with a
money man, an executive producer, but it turned out that
he was an intermediary employed by a third party . . .

He was trying to shaft you?

No, not at all. They were good deals. It's just that we didn't know who we were dealing with . . . If anyone was being deceitful, it was Catherine. She'd been keeping me in the dark.

Doing deals behind your back?

Yeah. She'd been negotiating the sale of material that wasn't for sale.

Screwing you?

Well, no . . . She *thought* she was doing me a favour. She'd got onto a colossal deal, and she figured it would be best if she handled it herself. It wasn't as if she intended to tear off with the money . . .

I'm sorry. You've lost me.

It came to a head one Friday night . . . We had tickets for the theatre, and Catherine got home late. Ridiculously late. I was angry enough already, but she made me even more angry by refusing to take my anger seriously. She said that she'd been caught up with something really big at the office. A fax had come in from Hollywood. She said that Steven Spielberg was ready to make a deal . . .

The *Steven Spielberg?* . . .

Absolutely . . . Spielberg was the silent party. The money.

That's fantastic!

That's what I said. But then Catherine told me that I should sit down, because the deal wasn't about what I thought it was about . . . She told me that Steven Spielberg wanted to make a film about my life.

She'd been selling your life story?

She said that she'd told Spielberg about my life, and he was very excited by it. She'd sent him a thirty-page treatment. Spielberg was willing to pay two million for the rights . . .

You're kidding me!

That's what I said. I said, this is fantastic, Steven Spielberg wants to make a film about *my* life . . . He's going to pay *two million dollars* for the rights to make a film about my life! And Catherine's rushing around the room saying how enthusiastic Steven is, that he's never been so excited. She's waving around her arms saying that not even Schindler excited him so much . . .

But?

Well, yes . . . *but* . . .

But what?

She said that Steven Spielberg was *incredibly* enthusiastic about the whole project, but there was just one thing . . .

. . . he wanted to cast Richard Dreyfus in the lead . . .

Worse than that.

Something could be worse than that?

There was just one thing that Spielberg wanted to change . . .

Oh, no . . .

I said, What do you mean, 'one thing that he wants to change'? . . . And she said, it's just one little thing . . . And I said, Yes, but *what* little thing? And Catherine looked at me, and she stopped smiling then, and I could see her eyes getting wet, and she said, Richard, this is the chance of a lifetime . . . Steven says that he's happy to run with the obsessions and repetitions, the disappearing women and the pathos and the approximations. He might even fork out for a computer-generated Marlon Brando . . . And I said, *what* little thing? . . . And she said, Steven really is *incredibly* enthusiastic about your life and its commercial potential, but . . . He wants to change the ending.

Acknowledgments

I don't subscribe to the auteur theory of authorship, and this book could not have been written without the assistance and encouragement of many people.

I am particularly indebted to my parents and family for their love and support.

I am most grateful to Gerald Murnane, and my fellow writing students at Deakin University for their critical advice. Thanks also to Paul Thompson and the staff of the Writing Department at AFTRS in Sydney, to Jenny Lee at *Meanjin* and Laura Danckwerts at *Ulitarra*.

I must also thank the following for their specific editorial assistance: James and Penny, Doug and Nan, Gus and The Braidottis, Dena, Sonia, Peter and Judy, Elise and Greg, Kate, Dr Doust, Philippa, Ben, Lisa, Niall, Dan, Robert and Louise, Jane, John, Gary, Clare, Fiona, Sally and Anne, Meaghan and Francis, Teresa, Anne, Andrew, Rose, Caroline, Polly, Sophie and Ariane.

Special thanks to Phil Jackson for the typewriter.

The following stories have been previously published: 'Marlon Brando' and 'Time and Motion' first appeared in

Verandah. 'A Letter to Francesca' first appeared in *Meanjin*. 'Motion Sickness', 'Extracts from *The Creative Process*', and 'The Correspondence School' first appeared in *Ulitarra*. 'The Leisure Society' was published in *The Age*.

THE HOUSE OF BALTHUS
David Brooks

'Deeply satisfying and sensually poetic . . . a
house readers will want to visit again and
again.'

Christopher Bantick, *Canberra Times*

The House of Balthus is a magical novel
which has the intensity of a dream.
Characters from the artist Balthus' paintings
walk out of the canvas and take on a life of
their own, sharing the spaces of an ancient
chateau now turned apartment block in a
large French provincial town. The concierge
Mme Lecault watches closely her tenants,
among them the Countess, the Professor, the
Painter, Therese and her young lover
Michael—but knows only the surface of their
lives. She spends her sleepless nights talking
to Mme Berry, who lives, it would appear, in
another century.

There is the sound of sobbing, which echoes
between rooms and across years; there is
desire stretched so taut the page seems to
vibrate with it, and the pain of lives where
desire is no longer allowed.

1 86373 912 2

IN TRANSLATION
Annamarie Jagose

'She writes like a dream . . . extraordinary
originality.'

Evening Post

'Passionate, full of erotic yearning.'

Metro

Helena begins an affair with the renowned
translator, Navaz Nicholson, and travels with
her to India, a country she never fully
understands. Abandoned by Navaz, a strange
pride will not allow Helena to return home
and she maintains anonymous contact with
her lover by intercepting instalments of the
Japanese novel Navaz is translating.
Rewriting at first a word here, a phrase
there, she finally takes over completely,
writing the novel's love triangle beyond its
original ending.

But there are more than words to Helena's
life. There is Lillian, the performance artist
who takes off a disguise only to assume
another, her aunt who sends postcards of
herself from around the world, Prakash, her
Indian tour guide and the mysterious
Professor Mody with his penchant for erotic
Haiku.

1 86373 962 9